# STONE OF THIEVES

## DIANE J. REED

Bandits Ranch Books

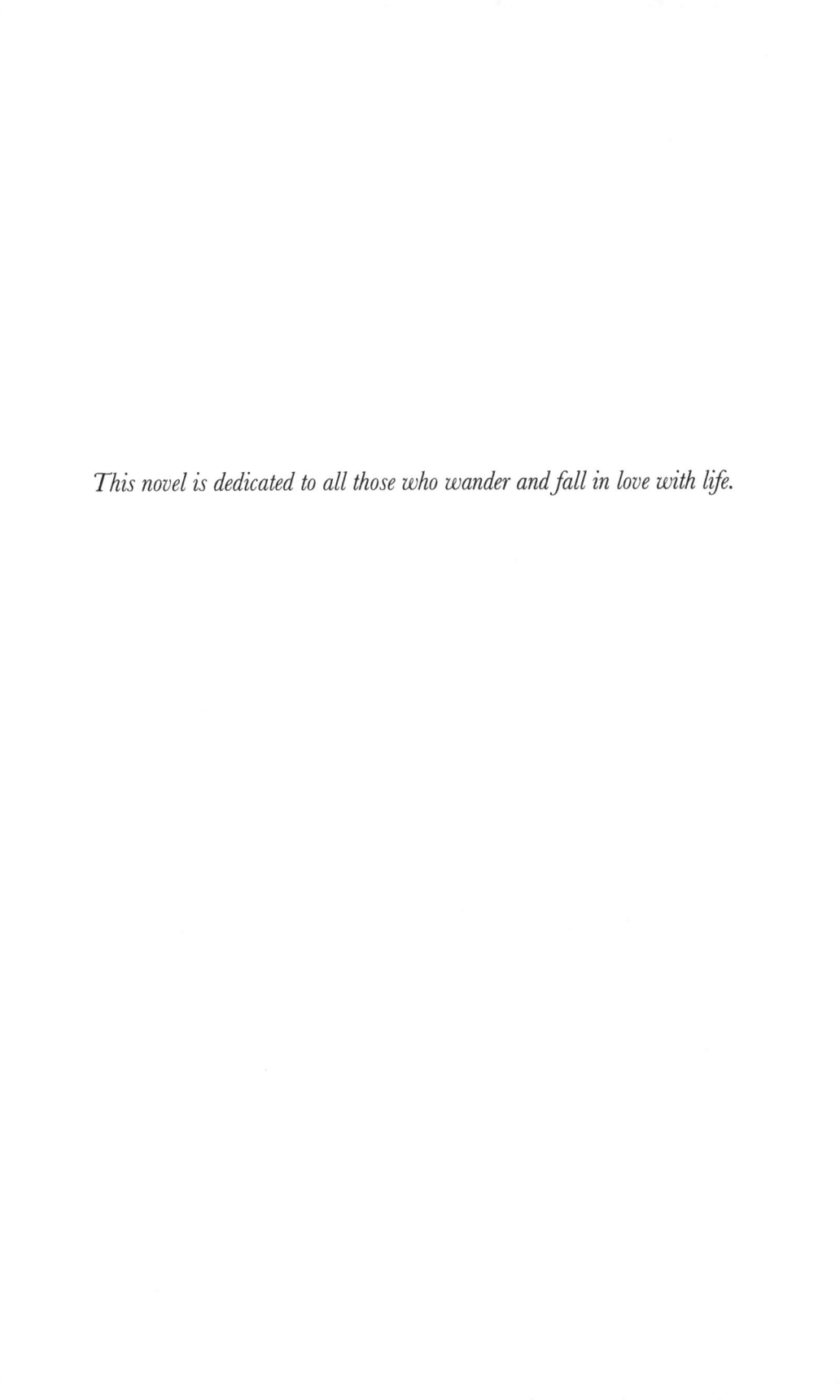

*This novel is dedicated to all those who wander and fall in love with life.*

I wake to the smell of blood.

Metallic, like maybe copper or iron, mixed with something fleshy and raw.

And eternal—

It calls to me.

Pulls me in the way a thief is drawn to an open drawer of jewels. Certain as the sparkle on a diamond or the heady aroma of a priceless perfume.

I remain still, my eyes closed, just taking in the scent.

Somewhere between dream and reality, this intoxicating smell invites me, as if wanting to carry me away in the flow of its deep red river. For a second, I feel myself go under, and I wonder if I've fallen into that crimson infinity…

But when I shake my head and glance up, I spy my boyfriend Creek in the airplane seat next to me with relief. He's sleeping, his cheeks soft and slack as a child, gold hair skimming his shoulders, his skin rich with that impossibly sun-kissed glow. Yet his stern jaw and fierce cheekbones make him look like a protective angel. Beautiful, sculpted right from a Renaissance master's dream.

But Creek's no angel—

And there's blood dripping down his arm.

Blood from a knife carved into his flesh by my own hand. Right before we got on the plane.

*Partners.*

That's the word he had me slice into his skin, more permanent than any tattoo. And a hell of a lot more enduring than the name of that blue-inked bitch he scratched out, now a long-forgotten scar.

You see, I stole his heart.

And he stole mine, too.

We're thieves. That's what we do.

ATMs, bank vaults, carefully-stashed lockboxes—these were our repertoire, until I discovered I'd inherited a fortune from my father's secret Swiss bank account that he'd registered in my name.

My *real* name.

Not Robin McArthur, like I'd thought all my life, but Rubina de Bargona. The bastard child of my white trash father's liaison with a pasta sauce heiress from Venice, Italy.

And that's exactly where we're headed right now.

Venice—the city of masks. An enigma within an enigma, floating precariously upon the blue-green waters of the Adriatic Sea.

Why?

Because Creek says I need to find my mother. My *real* mother, in order to find myself and steal back my history. She may be a nun, a drunk, or she may even be dead. But whatever I find, Creek says it will return a little piece of my soul back to me.

And he should know all about shattered pieces of soul, because his own mother was murdered in the backwoods trailer park outside of Cincinnati where we met. Where we tried to provide for our hard luck neighbors the only way we knew how: by stealing.

Now, there's no more need for taking what's forbidden—except for the truth of who I really am. And something tells me it won't come easy. Because the de Bargona family was so ashamed of my existence that they farmed me out for an adoption before returning to their ancestral home in Venice for good.

But my daddy stole me back.

After all, we come from a long line of thieves.

In the middle of the night, he broke into my adoptive family's house, grabbed me from my crib, and then changed our names and started a whole new life built on lies. Lies that both kept us together and tore us apart—until he couldn't hide the past from me anymore.

I glance at Creek again, at the blood that seeps through his black t-shirt and trickles down his forearm, where it fans out in rivulets as though his arm were sculpted from cracked pieces. A warm light from the window settles across his hard cheekbones, illuminating his stunning features. It still blows me away how much Creek loves me. How he took me under his wing—an angry chick on the lam—and taught me how to care about the people at the trailer park as much as I value my own life. His love stripped away everything I thought I knew, left me bare and gasping, and brought me back to the truth of my own soul—the only thing that Creek says ever really matters.

Grabbing some napkins wedged into the crease of my seat, I somehow manage to mop up the streams of blood dripping down his arm without stirring him from sleep. Impulsively, I can't help curling a finger along a thick strand of his messy hair that rests on his shoulder, relishing its feral wave that I've now streaked with a hint of red. I want to care for him, the way Creek often risked his life to care for me, as tenderly as a treasured child. But what to do with *Delta* napkins that look like they've witnessed a crime scene? I scan the nearby passengers, hoping no one noticed, and zip open my backpack to tuck them in. There, in the small outer pocket, is the faded news article of my mother from the *Cincinnati Enquirer* that my dad kept all these years. My heart wriggles into my throat. Despite my blood-stained fingers, I pull out the photo before the napkins can taint her image.

And it's like looking into a mirror.

Okay, so Alessia de Bargona is in a prim, white ball gown that makes her appear every inch the European debutante—a teenager who'd been biding her time at finishing school before her parents got the chance to arrange a politically advantageous wedding. But her hair is a long mass of dark curls, like mine, and her doe eyes are murky pools with that same bottomless wondering in them—as if she, too, was always searching for who she really is.

I'm so curious about her real personality, as opposed to this scared looking, candy-wrapped girl who bore me at only sixteen. How did she escape the Pinnacle Boarding School to have secret rendezvous' with my father, a mere stock boy at her dad's international pasta sauce plant? When she was away from the demands of society, did she laugh easily? Did she let her hair tumble to her shoulders and run barefoot through meadows by my dad's trailer park, smiling and picking daisies? She must have met Granny Tinker and all the other folks at Turtle Shores who loved her so. Trembling a little, I pull out the priceless ruby heart that Alessia had slipped into my dad's hand the day her father forced her to walk up to him and declare that she *never* loved him, and they were returning back to Venice.

My dad didn't believe her then.

And he cherished this jewel as his one true and shining hope that their love would last forever, and we'd someday find her again.

Has that someday finally come?

I gaze at my red-stained fingers, holding Alessia's picture in one hand and the ruby heart in the other.

And I swear to God, the ruby feels like it's getting warmer and heavier in my palm, pulsing even. Maybe it's my imagination. But as I stare closer at the cracks and fissures at its center, wondering how such a flawed ruby could possibly be considered "priceless," or whether it's just another one of my dad's lies, I have an overwhelming urge to lift my fingers to my lips. And to lick off Creek's blood.

But that's crazy.

Even so, I can't help feeling a magnetic connection, as if Creek's blood is like some kind of conduit to his very soul. The ruby in my hand seems to throb at the thought, and I slip the photo of my mother back into my backpack and cradle the gem in both hands. From somewhere deep inside the stone, I thought I heard a strange, lilting whisper.

*Taste it.*

I want to shake my head, throw down this spooky gem on the armrest between me and Creek and run to the restroom to quickly wash my hands.

But I can't—

All I can do is focus on the crimson facets of light that sparkle inside this ruby, mesmerized. And then I hear that whisper again.

*Your soul is marked.*

The pulses of the ruby fall into synch with my own heartbeat.

*Taste your destiny, Rubina—*

Without realizing it, I've brought my fingers to my lips.

For Christ's sake, I haven't had sex with Creek yet! We're just two teens who've only known each other for a few months, and spent most of that time operating incognito on the lam. He's never even had the chance to tell me his real last name.

But none of that can stop the overwhelming urge I have right now to sample Creek's blood. To swirl it around on my tongue and relish the taste the same way some women brag about abandoning themselves to orgasms. The pull of the life force that courses through his veins reels me in. Hesitantly, despite all rational thought, I take a lick—

And that's when I hear a woman's laughter echo in waves.

Followed by a scream.

And everything turns red.

She slaps him.

*Hard—*

The man in a black cape and mask takes a step back, teetering to recapture his balance from the force of her blow.

In a shaft of moonlight in a forest glen, I see him brace himself for a moment and struggle to stand a little taller. He rips off his mask to reveal a deeply handsome face, framed by dark wayward hair and caramel skin. His lips slip into a wry smile.

"Think you can get rid of me so easily?" he taunts the elegant woman in what I believe to be Italian, but for some reason I can understand him in English.

The woman is breathtakingly beautiful in her crimson, Renaissance-style ball gown with a matching feathery mask, her face framed by wild, black curls. On her delicate feet are curious, red embroidered shoes set atop tall, wooden platforms.

"Tonight," the man vows, "you're no rich man's whore. You are *mine.*"

Boldly, he steps forward and sinks his face into her pale, uplifted bosom.

The woman throws her dark hair back and clutches at him, her fingers raking through his curls as though clawing her way to his heart. They sway, as if in a dance, and the man in the black cape rips open the front laces of her dress, freeing her breasts to open air. Her nipples are erect, as if she'd been anticipating the caress of his tongue for hours.

"*Mia tesora,*" he breathes. His words hang in the air in small clouds of condensation. I can see the wet lines that shine in the moonlight as his tongue travels down her cleavage and circles her nipples.

It's cold outside—for some reason I sense the temperature but have no form, as though I'm made of vapor, like a ghost. Yet I can *see* everything in front of me in this secluded glen in the dead of winter, dotted with a lacy scattering of snow on the ground. Even so, I feel a hot blush rush up my being at watching the passion between these two lovers—the kind of sensual feast I've never tasted myself, yet I long for so desperately with Creek. The man knows this woman must be freezing, so he gallantly takes off his cape, revealing a gypsy shirt and trousers, and wraps it around her to cushion her fall. In one graceful arc, he lowers her to the forest floor before he tears open more laces and exposes the white skin of her belly and thighs. I watch his hand trace along her legs, gently massaging her skin as he fills her body with kisses.

When he starts swirling his tongue toward her sex, I'm far from shocked. Instead, beneath the delicate flickering of stars, I'm utterly transfixed by this sight, as though I've accidently stumbled upon something so forbidden and beautiful, it's—it's sacred.

Oh, what I would give if this were Creek and me right now...

Their passion is fierce and rises in thin wisps of steam from their bodies that curl in the frosty air. They're naked now, two starlit lovers at the height of their youth, and I can't help admiring her perfectly round breasts and the slim line of her waist that fits against his hard, sinewy chest as if they were two clasped hands. When he begins to pump into her, it's as though the earth itself trembles along with her waves of pleasure. I should be embarrassed, a former boarding school girl who's stumbled upon this mysterious dream like a voyeur. But the electricity of their desire sweeps me up in its power like a torrent of lightning-charged wind, almost as though it's happening to *me*. As the woman cries out in climax, her ecstasy filling the forest with a wild, raw sound, I see the man tear away her red feathered mask and toss it aside as though such an act were deflowering her far more than the prospect of burying his hot seed into her body.

The woman lifts her chin to him in defiance, and with a forceful sway of her hip, she expertly makes him come. As he does, and his groan rumbles across the ground, she tilts her head back and laughs.

"You couldn't stay away from me if you tried," she smiles.

It's then that I realize, with a start, that the woman looks exactly like *me*.

A searing light flashes across the glen, filling it with a white hot glow that burns my vision.

"Is this what you saw when you read my palm, my dear? Betrayal?"

The words cut across the forest as a man in a dark robe and a ghostly white mask sets down his lantern and holds up his hand. He traces his finger down a line on his palm.

"All those years ago, when you told me my fortune—did you plan your betrayal even then? Was that you I heard crying out in the forest for your dear children? Or was that the sound of something...*else?* Let's not keep them waiting at home any longer, shall we?"

The man strides over and stabs the woman's lover clean through the heart with a sword he'd hidden inside his robe. As her lover slumps to the ground, she shrieks and the sound echoes across the woods. The man holds his sword up to the moonlight. He points the sharp edge, dripping with blood, under the woman's chin and commands her to get up.

Still naked, her white skin gleaming under his lantern's glow, the woman quickly grabs something from her gown pocket and rises to her feet. She glares at him, unafraid with her perfect form in full display under the moonlight. Although tears stream down her cheeks, every curve of her breasts and hips seem to taunt him with their spellbinding power, and her eyes narrow in rage.

"Taste it!" The man shouts, shoving the point of his bloody sword to her lips. "Taste his *death*."

The woman laughs and sweeps her tongue across the tip with relish, then holds up a ruby heart that glistens in the moonlight.

"There's your mistake," she counters, ripping off his mask to reveal the old man's face. "Blood on blood lives forever, you fool. When a Gypsy Queen tastes her true love's blood, her powers only *grow*. Now you'll never be rid of me."

"Oh? I wouldn't be so certain—"

With that, the man grabs the ruby stone from her grip and slices his sword across her throat. Her body instantly drops to the ground, but a mist begins to gather over the blood on her neck, as if her soul has become a vapor and is seeping out of her body. It rises in the air in a swirl and heads for the stone in his hand.

Pulling me along with it!

Despite my own willpower, I feel her spirit tangle fiercely with mine in the night air, circling me like a hot funnel. Her determination is strong—much stronger than I can imagine—and it takes every ounce of my being to withstand against her as she aims for the cracks at the center of that ruby heart.

"Come with me, sweet gypsy!" she cries, somewhere between the fissures of time and space where only spirits seem to dwell. "Together, we can destroy him."

"No!" I protest, warring against her. I try to condense myself into icy crystals—anything to separate my energy from the force of her hot, steaming vitality. "I don't want to be absorbed by you!"

"Then what *do* you want?" she hisses in an accusatory tone, as though I've transgressed against her with some time-honored violation I know nothing about.

"I want Creek—"

"What is it baby?"

I blink several times, bewildered.

Creek's warm hands are around my cheeks, cradling my face. His thumbs gently stroke my skin as though I'm a lost little girl. "You were calling my name," he says. "Loudly."

The intense blue of his worried eyes soothes me after my red hot nightmare. They're the kind of icy beautiful that can knock you from your senses for a moment and erase all thought.

I shake my head, still foggy. "I-I must have had a bad dream."

Creek's concern only deepens. "But your eyes were *open*, Robin." He gazes at the ruby heart in my hands as if it might have germs. "You sure you're okay?"

"Yeah, of course." I try to make light of it, even though I'm completely perplexed. I toss the ruby into the front pocket of my backpack like a hot potato. "I ate so much greasy Skyline Chili back in Cinci before we left, it's a wonder I didn't hallucinate about Oompa Loompas."

I smile a little. Though Creek lets his hands fall from my face, I can tell he isn't fooled. I'm not about to admit to him that I actually tasted his blood on a bizarre whim. Is that the reason for my strange daytrip?

A cloud bank engulfs our airplane, surrounding us in a white haze like the weird vapor I'd become in my vision, and it gives me shivers. For some reason it feels as if we've rolled into infinity, where time doesn't obey the same rules anymore—and I feel like my whole identity on this plane is up for grabs. I know I've gone from Robin McArthur to Robin McCracken to Rubina De Bargona in the span of only three short months. And yeah, maybe that's traumatic. But this seems deeper, like something at a soul level has shifted. I don't know why, but I feel older now, and a whole lot more world weary than my 16 years.

Peering at my backpack, I spot the wooden bluebird that Granny Tinker had whittled for me as a gift before I left the trailer park, and I pluck it from a side pocket for comfort the way a child reaches for a stuffed toy. Stroking its carefully carved wings, I notice it doesn't look like the usual bluebirds that hung around Turtle Shores. It's shaped more like a hawk, and she stained its claws bright red. A bit odd, but then there's no deciphering Granny Tinker's strange web of superstitions. When I cradle the bird in my palm, I can feel it has a little trap door on its belly with a tiny hinge that I hadn't noticed before. Pushing it open with my finger, a slip of paper drops out. I unfurl it and read the inscription in Granny Tinker's awkward hand.

April 1, 1996 Queen of the Gypsies
I done told ya yer soul was marked.
Beware of threes.

Immediately, my forehead grows hot.

That date is my birthday—

But it's two years *older* than when my daddy told me I was born.

Oh God.

Could Granny Tinker be trying to expose another one of my dad's lies?

It would explain why I always did better than the other kids at school, without hardly studying. And why I was the first of my girlfriends to reach my full height and get my period in only the 5$^{th}$ grade—not to mention a training bra by then. But why now? Why did Granny Tinker bother to tell me this for my trip, and what the hell does she mean by Queen of the Gypsies?

"Creek," I blurt angrily. "How old are you? Really? And don't you dare lie to me—"

Creek squints his eyes, in that cool way he always used to do before sizing up any threats at one of our bank jobs. His face muscles tighten, strong jaw working slowly over molars. He's not one to give up information easily, but I believe he trusts me. Then again, he's never told me his full name, age, where he was born, who is father was—nothing. His jaw shifts a little and his eyes search mine, as though weighing the risk to *me* if I know too much about him. Then his gaze travels over the dried smear of blood that stains his arm.

"You told me we were *partners*," I remind him. "It says so on your arm." I swallow hard, going for the kill now. "You also told me you love me."

Creek's eyes lock on mine.

God, he can be cold!

I hardly know who Creek is sometimes. He's like a dark continent that's been only partially mapped, because no one's ever been brave enough to try and enter that deep interior.

I draw a breath, my heart lurching a beat.

Except me.

I'm that brave and he damn well knows it. I've proven it on bank jobs, and I wonder if this is a make or break time for us. Raising my chin, I stare him down. I don't give a shit if there's things about his life he doesn't want to reveal. He knows everything about me—as much as I do, anyway—and I'm gonna make damn sure this relationship stays a two-way street.

And that's when I see a sly smile toy at Creek's lips. The jagged scar on his cheek crinkles into a straight line, like a dagger, which always manages to pierce my heart.

This is exactly why he loves me, and I know it.

Creek surprises me with a kiss, his lips tender and moist and so thoroughly absorbed, it's as if he could inhale me right now. My hands instinctively seek out his chest, roaming over the contours of his hard muscles. Our breaths sync, chests rising as one. I feel his warm palm slip behind my neck and finger a cowlick, stroking so softly I could purr. He cradles my head like I'm precious to him. I guess this is our relationship in a nutshell. I'm the only one who stands up to Creek's ice, and he's the only one who can practically drown me in his hotness, making everything else fall away…

Oh yeah, and he'd kill anybody who tries to mess with me.

When he breaks from our kiss, without a word, Creek pulls a passport from his back pocket and tosses it onto my lap.

I open it up. It reads, *John Corrigan, May 3, 1996.* Today is only May 1st, so he's still 17 years old?

I whip out my passport too, feeling flustered that I hadn't checked it out yet. It states, *Lisa Harris, April 1, 1998.* That means 16 years old.

"But these are fake," I remind him, glancing at the phony names, although the birthday is what I used to think was correct for me. Creek said he'd gotten the passports from one of his backwoods underworld connections, the same guys who fenced my stolen car when we discovered it had a tracer. Sucking up my courage, I show him the snippet of paper from Granny Tinker's bluebird, and watch his eyes grow wide.

So Creek didn't know I'm 18 either!

His Adam's apple chases up and down his throat.

"Granny would never lie to you," he concedes.

And I know it's the truth. If anything, she specializes in telling you what you *don't* want to hear in an infinite number of spooky ways. I curse under my breath. I don't know what makes me madder, the fact that my dad duped me yet *again*, or the fact that I could have had sex with Creek by now without a shred of guilt.

But wait a minute—Creek was born in May? He's a month *younger* than I am at 17?

I can't resist elbowing him. "So how does it feel to be jailbait, *partner?*"

Creek's frigid stare is a swift reminder of just how old his soul really is—one part lethal and another part forever untamed. It's moments like this that scare me to the bone, and I have to wonder about what went on in his childhood that splintered his heart into such razor-edged pieces. Still, Creek didn't learn to respect me because I back down easily, and I'm not going to wimp out now.

Feeling cold, I wrap a thin Delta blanket around me and curl myself as best I can into the airplane seat, then boldly rest my head on Creek's shoulder to keep up the pretense that he never rattles me.

"Sweet dreams—*John*," I say with a smirk, hoping to make him lighten up. I feel indescribably tired, and I need to get more sleep before we arrive in Venice tonight. "What a shame you're a minor and you can't buy alcohol in Italy."

As I let my eyes fall closed, Creek gives my nose a tweak.

"Based on your passport, you can't either—*Lisa*."

I laugh a little at myself and cuddle up against him, heaving a sigh. "Oh well, guess that means we'll have to do what we always do."

"Which is…" replies Creek.

"Steal it."

## ❧ 3 ❧

Creek's sinewy arms are wrapped around me, softened by his flannel overshirt, as my eyes flutter open from a hard sleep. There's nothing I want more right now than to linger in his embrace forever. The firmness of his chest feels like home to me—a haven I've never really had before. But when a moist breeze begins to caress my cheeks, fragrant with the exotic scent of jasmine and bougainvillea, I perk up and glance around. What I see before me rises straight out of a dream. An indigo lagoon stretches to an open sea, with the glow of street lights shimmering in its waters and narrow boats swaying at its edges like delicate slippers. Blinking several times, I sit up straight and gasp. The majestic silhouettes of Old World buildings on either side of the canal make me feel as if we've entered a fairy tale…

"Something tells me we aren't in O-Ohio anymore," I mutter breathlessly.

Creek's warm lips nuzzle against my neck.

"Congratulations, baby—this is Venice," he whispers. "The world your family really comes from."

I shudder, feeling as if he'd just placed a gold crown upon my head.

But then I remember that I'm illegitimate—and pretty much the last person on earth the de Bargonas want to meet.

"W-where do we go from here?" I ask Creek. It's not like we'd had time to plan an itinerary for this trip.

"Bridge of Sighs," breaks in a man with a thick Italian accent I hadn't noticed before.

Whipping around, I see a portly, bearded guy behind us with a gold gypsy ring in his ear bearing a long oar that he stirs into the water from our gondola. *Gondola?* It's then that I vaguely recall getting off the airplane and onto a train that shuttled us here. I must have fallen asleep again—so Creek *carried* me onto this boat? I search Creek's eyes. He merely gives me a wink.

"*Ponte del Sospire,*" our gondolier insists, turning our boat to the left and pointing at a small bridge over a canal. Its pale stones reflect a golden hue from the setting sun that's a little eerie highlighted against the deep azure of the twilight-colored water. "This bridge is both the beginning and the end for Venezia."

"What do you mean?" I ask.

He digs in his oar and swivels our boat, where we see the last fiery swaths of gold and crimson streak across the sky at sunset.

"Now we wait," he says with a smile.

The tide gently swells and subsides, tossing our boat a little, and then soft bells begin to echo across the water.

"*La campanile de San Marco,*" our gondolier nods. "Legend has it that if you kiss your beloved as the sun goes down to the ringing of the bells, your love will last forever."

Creek doesn't miss his chance.

He sweeps me up in a luscious kiss before the bells cease, his fingers gripping my jaw like he means it. His skin still smells musky and wild, like the brambly forest around Bender Lake where we met, tinged with the sharpness of smoke and something else—something as mysterious and raw as one of Granny Tinker's magic candles. As the bells of San Marco begin to fade, his lips break away and he tilts his forehead against mine. I can feel his warm breath stroke my cheeks. And those eyes—as stunning as a glacier and just as forbidding sometimes. But right now, their cool depths look into mine as if I might open the way to his idea of eternity. With one last stolen kiss, he smiles and turns to gaze at the sunset that takes both our breaths away.

"Here we are at crossroads," our gondolier says. "The Bridge of Sighs either brings eternal love," he points to the open sea, and then back to the city of Venice, "or was the last stop for prisoners before jail. Which one do you choose?" He looks at me in a manner that makes me nervous. "Either way," he continues, "you are bound to sigh. Love and loss—they are destiny."

The gondolier gazes at me knowingly. I realize this sounds coo-coo, but I can't help wondering if he knows I'm a thief—that Creek and I are both thieves—and we could easily belong to either future. The thought makes me uneasy, and I change the subject.

"Do you, um, know any places we can stay in the area?"

The gondolier remains quiet, sizing me up. Finally, he nods his head.

"You want to pay a fortune," he says, gesturing at a palatial, tangerine building to our left that's so elegant, it's beyond my wildest dreams. "You knock on the door of Hotel Danieli." I see a smile play at his lips. "But if you want to feel at home, you go to my family's bed and breakfast on the island of Burano. They feed you well."

"Danieli," Creek pipes up. I know he doesn't give a damn about creature comforts. It's anonymity he's after—the gondolier's wife might remember our faces.

"Very well," our gondolier sighs, staring at the bridge up ahead. He rows us to a platform and expertly parks our boat parallel to the walkway. "*Ciao*, my lovers."

Creek pays him handsomely from the wad of cash in his backpack that he brought on this trip. And no sooner do we step off the gondola onto dry land than we're accosted by a gypsy woman selling flowers.

"*Fiore!*" she shouts aggressively, shoving her blooms at us with a gap-toothed smile. "*Bella fiore!* Euro—pound—dollar!"

I sneeze at the bouquet of wildflowers she stuffed into my face. I vaguely recall being warned before leaving our train to watch out for gypsy vendors who haunt the shadows of Venice, specializing in distraction while they pick your pockets. Swiftly, I take off my backpack and remove the ruby heart and slip it into the front pocket of my jeans, where it will be harder to snatch. Just then, the gypsy woman drops her bouquet to the ground. The colorful petals scatter across the sidewalk like confetti.

"No…" she gasps, barely above a whisper.

She studies my face as though reading my aura and mutters something in what I guess to be her gypsy tongue. At the sound of her lilting voice, I swear the ruby heart in my pocket begins to grow warm and throbs.

"*Thagarni?*" the gypsy woman asks, her body visibly shaking. She eyes me warily as if she'd seen a ghost. Before I know it, she's fallen to her knees and is pulling out coins from her skirt pocket and arranging them in a peculiar star pattern at my feet. They shine under the streetlamp like burnished gold.

"What the hell are you doing?" I protest, flabbergasted. "I can't take your money—"

Undaunted, the woman mumbles a phrase over and over that I don't understand like a series of Hail Mary's. Her tone is peculiar, as though she's petitioning for something. All at once, I hear a loud pop. A streak of fire rips through my hair and grazes across the side of my head like the fingers of a warm lover—

"Robin, get down!" Creek orders.

He pulls me to street level so fast that my cheek meets the cobblestones with a hard thud and sends shockwaves through my brain. Dragging me by the shoulders across the street with lightning speed, Creek covers me and becomes a blur as I scramble to find my feet and keep up with him. My lungs are on fire and my heart is hammering so fast I fear it will explode. With the strategic swiftness of a seasoned criminal, Creek locates a dark alley and throws my body against a wall in shadows.

"Keep your head down!" he commands as I hear another bullet whistle by.

It's then that I realize what we're really up against—someone is deliberately shooting at us. As in, they want us dead.

And Creek doesn't cower for a second.

He leaps like a phantom from our dark alley corner and jumps the man stupid enough to peek his head into the entryway with a gun in his hand. The two become one writhing creature on the ground until I see Creek manage to rise on top and pin the man down. Their hands struggle fiercely for control of the man's gun.

"Creek!" I cry, horrified at what I'm witnessing. Within seconds, Creek has the man's pistol and aims it straight at his forehead. His instant finesse at handling this weapon shocks me—obviously, this isn't his first gunfight. I can hear the cold metal sound the pistol makes as he cocks the trigger, punctuated by the man's panicked breaths.

In a slim shaft of light from a nearby streetlamp, I see the thug gazing at Creek as if he's God. The veins at his temple bulge at the surface of his skin, appearing ready to burst.

"Who do you work for!" Creek demands, giving him a shake.

The man squeezes his eyes tight and seals his lips into a thin line, offering up no information. He trembles wildly as though prepared to meet his Maker. A shrill whistle blows, and I hear shouts that sound like Italian police.

"Creek, the police are coming—they'll help!" I insist, not wanting to see blood splattered all over us at Creek's doing.

"No!" Creek replies, and to my utter astonishment, he lets the thug go.

In a fleeting second, they guy scrambles from beneath

Creek and makes a mad dash into the shadows of the alleyway, stumbling several times but then vanishing like a greased rat. With a flick of his wrist, Creek throws the pistol into a dark crevice between crumbling buildings that's pooled with a foot of tidewater. Then he grabs me and yanks me to my feet, swallowing me in a kiss so forceful I fear I'm about to be devoured.

At that moment, two policemen appear in the alleyway. They shine blinding flashlights at us—a couple of lip-locked lovers who now look like any ordinary tourists out for a romantic stroll in the city of Venice. Nothing unusual...

"*Contiuare!*" One policeman barks to the other in a huff.

As Creek's hand rises to my breasts like a half-starved lover, the beams of their flashlights flit across the alley. Then their lights scan a series of criss-cross lines through the darkness and slowly disappear.

## ✳ 4 ✳

We gaze up at the night sky.

Creek's arm is raised in the dark and he's fingering the rim of a constellation, tracing the twinkling spires of a star…

Just like the one the gypsy woman arranged with her coins at my feet.

It makes me tremble.

He pulls the canvas up to our chests like one of Granny Tinker's quilts. But it's really the fabric cover over an old gondola in need of repair, tucked into the shadows of a forgotten canal archway.

We're here because Creek doesn't trust anyone. Not the local police or even the staff at nearby hotels. Anybody can be crooked, he says—for the right *price*. And if they leak our whereabouts, we might not be lucky enough to escape next time.

He slips his arm beneath me and holds me tight. This

place, this dark sanctuary in the heat of his embrace, makes me feel like I've fallen down a hole and melted to become a permanent part of his skin.

And that's when I let the tears fall.

They trickle down my cheeks and onto his shoulders, but I'm still too frightened to make a sound. I'm shaking all over. He strokes my hair long and slow.

"Shhh, baby," he whispers, rocking me like a child. "I've got you now. And I'm never letting go."

He pulls a white feather from his jeans pocket and holds it up, luminous in the moonlight, and presses his cheek against mine.

It's all we've got left.

Our backpacks are gone. There wasn't time to grab them again in the confusion—we were fortunate to get out alive.

So this is the sum of what we have: each other, a white feather, and a ruby heart.

And not another penny to our names.

Kind of ironic for a couple of thieves.

Creek sits up on his elbows and brushes his lips against my forehead, tender and soft as an angel. He takes his white feather and traces a point above my brows, then draws it over my cheekbones and down to my lips in the shape of a star. He's so close I can feel the moisture of his breath. I want to fuck him right now—fuck him hard to make me forget the horror of what just happened. Grind his bones and muscles together with such force that we ignite into some kind of incandescent, shining thing, and he'd never guess in a million years that I'm a virgin. But the way Creek is gazing at me in this moment isn't lust. It's…

Fear.

A kind of dread I've never seen in his eyes before. And it doesn't look like it's for himself. It's for *me*—

I don't get it. Those bullets could have made Creek just as dead.

Creek's feather sweeps across my cheeks, first the right side and then the left, wiping away my tears like a silent gift. It's the feather he always used to pray with to the spirit of his mother. The one Granny Tinker says he used to conjure me all the way from Cinci to help him provide for the folks at Turtle Shores. I know it might sound crazy, but that feather is by far the most precious thing Creek owns.

"What happened, baby?" he says, his voice so low it reminds me of a purr.

"H-how the hell should I know?" I gasp, still trembling. "Why would anyone want us dead?"

"Not us." Creek shakes his head. "*You*. They had plenty of chances to shoot me, Robin. *You're* the one they're after. Now tell me what happened."

I bite my lip, just as bewildered by the whole incident as he is.

Creek sighs, growing a little impatient. He wriggles his hand into my jeans pocket and pulls out the ruby heart. "I don't mean in the back alley—I mean on the airplane. With this stone. You saw something, baby, I know it. I could feel the change in you just as sure as a shift in the wind." He turns over the stone in the moonlight, making its facets subtly glisten. "And that something means more to certain people than your *life*."

All breath escapes me.

Creek's talking about that strange vision I had? I don't see how my random hallucination connects with a thug who was shooting at us.

"Robin," Creek persists, "ordinary street punks don't carry guns around that can land their asses in jail for a decade. They snatch and run about a million times a day—it's all a numbers game. That guy was willing to *die* rather than tell me who he works for. And I guarantee that means he works for someone incredibly powerful, or else he would have lied and bolted for the gutter. Get it? Somebody wants something from you. And I have a hunch it's this stone. Now tell me what you *saw*."

I swallow hard. I know Creek's radar about underworld types has been honed to perfection. He's like a wolf when it comes to smelling their moves—and their motives. There's no escaping his eerie accuracy, so I nod my head.

"Okay, I was simply holding the ruby," I finally relent. "I know you're gonna think this is weird, but I'd been wiping off your arm, so I had your blood on my hands. Then I heard a voice. Just a whisper, but it kept telling me to lick my fingers."

I glance into Creek's eyes, waiting for some acknowledgement that I've gone batshit crazy. Instead his expression seems stern in the moonlight, and I hear him hold his breath.

Like maybe he's actually...*believing* me?

"Creek, the second I tasted your blood, *pow*. I found myself in another time, only I wasn't the same me. I was more like vapor. I saw these two lovers in winter who had Renaissance clothing on and masks, like for Mardi Gras. I'm pretty sure they were speaking Italian, but for some reason, I could understand them in English. A man discovered them—the woman's husband—and he killed them both. But when he got to the woman and cut her throat, she somehow sent her soul into this ruby."

Creek remains silent.

His stunning silhouette is motionless in the darkness, a carved stone.

I feel his chest against mine, slowly taking in another breath.

But he says nothing.

Even so, I can feel the muscles in his biceps begin to tighten and twitch, his chest as hard as a marble slab.

I know this feeling. It's when Creek snaps back into work mode, protective yet aloof as ice—and at the same time incendiary as a match, every muscle in his being ready to fire into action.

But action toward what?

He's that dark continent again, restless and impossible to read.

"Creek, what does this all mean?" I press, grasping his shoulders and shaking him a little. It's useless, I know, like trying to rattle a wall. So I boldly grab the stone back from his fist.

"Maybe this is just a stupid rock," I point out in a flat tone to hide my panic, half-tempted to chuck it into the canal. "And I simply had a bad dream. Maybe we shouldn't be running all over Venice to find my mom if it puts us in danger with a bunch of street swindlers—"

"Oh baby," Creek's deep voice rolls as gently as the Adriatic Sea. His fingers stroke the line near my temple where the bullet grazed my head. Until that moment, I hadn't realized it had left a mark. "We're in danger now no matter what we do. As good as fucking dead. Don't you see that?"

He cups my face and kisses me so fiercely it makes my tears return. Like a man who might not see me in the morning—or ever again. The rawness of his skin against mine, our sweep of tongues melding with his lips hot and violent, makes me tremble all the way to my core. I'm not sure, but I think both our mouths are bleeding.

"Listen to me, Robin," he cuts away, fighting for breath, "I say, fuck 'em. Whoever wants this stone is gonna have to chase us all over Italy. Because we're shadows, Robin—we are night. And we don't give in. No matter what happens, we're going find your mother if it's the last thing we do. You understand?"

I nod my head tentatively, scared as hell.

Creek crushes me in his arms, too tight, but I want it this way. He feels like he's trying to cocoon me into his soul for safety, and God as my witness, if I could crawl inside his chest right now, I would. He brushes—bruises—my neck with another piercing kiss. I can taste his blood lingering on my lips. And I feel like the very smell of him, blood and sweat and soul of him, has somehow trickled into my bones. His taste, his scent, it swirls in my brain, a hot explosion of neuro-napalm. It's molten and it's now, and it's exactly what I need.

Creek's hungry mouth slides down my throat, pressing a little too hard on my windpipe and nearly knocking the wind out of me. I don't care—he can have my air. His lips slide across my collarbone and seek the swell of my breasts, burrowing into the soft fold of my cleavage. I hear him inhale deeply, as if the scent of our skin on skin strengthens him— maybe fuses us together like scattered rays of light into one beam. It's then that he rests his head on my heart, which leaps at the press of his weight. I thread my fingers through his tangled hair, gripping fistfuls as if he's my lifeline.

Because he is.

"Robin," Creek whispers, breathless. He turns to stare up at the sky, at the star that had twinkled so brightly. "If we're destined to meet our Maker on this trip, and there's nothing we can do to change that, I want you whole in the afterlife. *All* of you. Because I will hunt you down and make you mine for eternity. Not a shattered soul like my mom, her heart shot to a million pieces. But someone who knows exactly who she is and what she wants. And who chooses me. Chooses *us*. And who never—ever—runs and hides."

I unravel the knots in Creek's hair with my fingers, bowled over by his words. I don't want him to know how hot and fast my tears are flowing right now. This kind of love is rare— maybe it only happens once in a lifetime, or within a whole generation of lifetimes. Or only to those whose fates are delicately inscribed in those stars…

And maybe the stone knows that.

Because ever since I've been holding it in my hand with Creek in my arms, it burns like a fire. It's so hot, it's everything I can do to not let it go.

And I don't know how to tell Creek that. All I want him to know is that I'm not giving up, either.

I choose *us*.

Leaning down, I press a kiss to his forehead, relishing the saltiness and hint of pine and charcoal on his skin. As I do, I hear a voice echo across the canal like a ghost. Glancing up, I see the silhouette of a boat in the distance with a gondolier singing like he's searching for a lost love. The ruby heart throbs in my hand.

"Creek," I ask, unsettled by my own question right now, but drumming up the courage to hold up the heart to the moonlight. For the first time, I notice the cracks at its center gleam like a star. "D-Do you think this ruby is somehow magic?"

Creek shakes his head in the darkness. He nestles deeper into my chest.

"No," he replies.

His arms hug me closer, and he's silent for what seems like forever.

But then I hear him take a deep breath.

"I think *you* are."

The morning sun in Venice lights the city on fire.

We lie exhausted in each other's arms inside the old gondola, with Creek still asleep on my chest.

I toy with his pale hair, savoring the way the strands unfurl through my fingers. The weight of him, rarely this relaxed and vulnerable, makes me feel like my arms hold the world.

But the red roof tiles of the antiquated buildings around us have begun to gleam with gold. I know this moment is fleeting, because before the day gets bright, we'll need to hit the convents in search of my mother. It's the only lead I have from my dad back at Bender Lake—the persistent rumor all these years that Alessia de Bargona was shipped off to a Venetian nunnery once she gave birth to me.

But we'll have to move in shadows.

Because I have no idea who wants me dead. Or who wants this ruby.

It couldn't be the de Bargonas—they don't even know I'm

here. And probably not the gypsies, or that flower lady would've tried to grab it last night instead of looking at me like an alien and creating a strange star from her coins. How would she know I was carrying it? How could *anyone* know?

Surely the nuns of Venice will be safe for me to question, at least about my mom.

But I'm not slipping a word about this stone.

All I'm interested in is a brief meeting with my real mother for some answers. Did she ever really love my dad? Did she perhaps miss me all these years?

My heart is made of armor.

I'm ready for a blank look in her eyes, as though she'd forgotten us both long ago. Or a shifting glance meaning the answer is no. That, too, is a kind of closure. Then Creek and I will bolt from Italy like a couple of birds on the wing. Hopefully *alive*.

I jiggle Creek and watch his ivory lashes flutter. He looks up at me with those striking eyes of frozen blue. When his vision comes into focus, he gives me that crooked smile that makes his cheek scar slip into the image of a dagger, and it snatches my breath from my throat.

Creek steals a kiss.

"Hey baby," he says softly.

But he's up in a flash—the way I knew he would be. All adrenaline before the day fully breaks. "Most criminals are lazy," he reminded me last night. "They sleep in late and do their dirty work in darkness. Right before dawn is the best time to make your moves."

Together, we smooth out the canvas over the gondola and shove it further beneath the archway like we were never there.

And I'm starving.

But I can't withdraw money at a bank because whoever's after me could see us or talk to tellers. Instead, we'll remain in alleyways and between crevices, slinking along the edges of buildings like stealthy cats.

Creek takes me by the hand and weaves me around the corners and nooks of this ancient city that's still asleep. The flowers on balcony planter boxes haven't opened their blooms to the sun yet, and the city is hushed. But to be honest, I love it this way. Compared to the gray, blocky industriousness of Cincinnati, it's a feast for the eyes and I'm overwhelmed at the grandeur. All around us is the delicate beauty of ornate yet crumbling buildings in pastel colors with green water lapping at their edges, as though the tide seeks to reclaim their souls to sea. Canal boats sway in the docks, and shops sit nestled with their bright shudders closed tight, as if still lost in dreams. The only thing I hear is the gentle chortle of pigeons searching for crumbs. But then a bell peals through the twilight haze of morning, just five rings, and in the distance I spy several gleaming crosses that rise over the city, indicating churches. As we continue to meander through tight alleys edged by lazy canal water, the ruby heart begins to wobble in my pocket. The closer we get to an old stone building with an arched door marked by a primitive cross, the more the ruby heart grows warm.

I stop in my tracks.

This wasn't the plan—

We were going to spend the morning knocking at as many religious institutions as we could find, showing them the old newspaper photo of my mother and asking if Alessia de Bargona ever lived there.

But the photo of my mom went the way of our backpacks.

And I didn't know the heart in my pocket might suddenly start acting as a compass.

Frozen, I wrap my arms around myself, completely weirded out again.

"What is it," Creek asks, pulling me into a dark gap between buildings where he knows we'll be safer. He folds his arms around me like wings.

"It's *her*," I reply, patting my pulsing jeans pocket. "Whatever her name really is. I think she's telling me where Alessia is—or used to be. At that old church up ahead."

Creek is quiet. He nods.

"You know, you *are* Granny Tinker's second cousin," he whispers. His lip lifts at the corner with a smile. "That means you're one part magic—and one part crazy."

I give him a punch to the ribs.

"Ow," he laughs. "It's true! Now c'mon—let's get this over with and meet your mom 'cause I'm hungry. If we time it right, we can finish up and still swipe some fruit and bread before the vendors start really watching."

Just as Creek says that, I spot a canopy rolling up at a nearby market. The smell of cheese floats strongly past us, and before I know it, I'm drooling. If it weren't for the stone beating insistently in my pocket, I would have dived to grab a hunk by now.

"*Focus.*" Creek gently grabs my shoulders, and we quietly move from shadow to shadow like snakes. When he sees the old church I mentioned, he guides me around the side to a door away from the street that looks as though it hasn't been opened in years.

And the stone burns like a coal in my pocket.

*Istituto de Santa Pellegrina* reads a chipped wooden plaque beside the door. I swear, it looks like it was carved centuries ago.

Drawing a deep breath, I peer into Creek's eyes for courage and raise my hand to the rusty, wrought-iron door knocker to give it a lift. It falls with a weighty boom that surprises us both.

And nothing happens.

Creek and I exchange glances. We know we can't afford to go to the front of the church. Whoever shot at us last night is hardly going to respect the public doorstep of a sacred building. I extend my fingers to give the door knocker another rap when Creek stops my hand.

Sure enough, we can hear the slow sound of shuffling feet.

Heart in my throat, I watch the faded mahogany door creak open.

She's a vision in all white, this woman who peeks at me through the crack. But her face is deeply lined and her brown eyes appear a bit cloudy.

"Alessia—is she here?" I gasp. I hear the desperate-child quality in my voice, fully betraying the earnest-daughter-searching-for-her-mother that I truly am. But I can't help myself.

The nun squints and looks us up and down with an impartial gaze.

And slams the door.

Before I can pound it with all my might, Creek's arms

clench around me like a straitjacket, his big hand over my mouth nearly suffocating me.

"Don't you *dare* holler," he growls.

In spite of my thrashing, I know this is for my own good—we can't afford to reveal where we are. But that doesn't stop me from biting his palm.

"Dammit!" Creek hisses barely above a whisper, waving his hand. "Can't you listen to me for one sweet second?"

My cheeks flush warm.

In the cold air of dawn, I see little puffs of my own breath escape like I'm an unruly dragon. Yet to my surprise, the heavy door creaks open again. Without glancing up, the same nun as before stuffs a crumpled wad of newspaper into my hands. Confused, I wonder if her mind is slipping a little, and she thinks we've come to collect the trash. But when I open the folds of paper I spy a large hunk of bread and wedge of cheese.

"*Dio ti benedica,*" the nun mumbles, crossing herself in routine fashion as if she's handed out food like this for charity a thousand times.

She obviously thinks we're hungry—and she's right.

But we didn't come for a meal.

"Please—Alessia?" I pipe up, while Creek thrusts his boot into the threshold before she can slam the door. He doesn't wince when the three-inch-thick wood smashes against his foot.

"A prayer!" He slaps his hands together, nodding intently before she can leave. Those arresting blue eyes of his could melt even the most cynical cleric. "You wouldn't leave us without a prayer, would you?"

Creek's words halt the old nun in her tracks. She stares at his sealed, upright palms, her face registering his request.

"*Un momento*," she sighs, leaving the door ajar this time as she shuffles down a hallway lined with gilded artwork depicting the Stations of the Cross. After she disappears into a side room, Creek and I stuff down the morsels she gave us like ravenous dogs, our tastebuds nearly bursting from the rich flavor of the cheese as we wait. In a few minutes, the old woman returns with another nun—a bare slip of a woman— who appears thirty years her junior. "*Inglese*," the old nun says to the other with a nod. But when the young nun sets eyes on me, her rosary drops to the floor. The small beads echo across the tile with a clatter.

"*Muerte*," she gasps. "Ali?"

The young nun's face blanches. Tears rim her eyes, and she looks as if she's holding herself back from giving me a hug.

"Ali—*Ali?*" she repeats, visibly trembling now. Timid, she holds out her hand and runs it down a strand of my curly dark hair. When her fingers stretch to the bottom, it springs back into place.

Could Ali be a nickname for Alessia? I wonder. Were they friends?

I want to tell her the answer is no. My name isn't Ali, it's Robin, or Rubina for that matter. But Alessia used to be—I mean *IS*—my mother. Except the stone's burning so hot in my front pocket right now that I can't talk. I have to pull it out before it blisters my skin and shift it into my back pocket where the jean fabric is thicker.

"Th-They told me you were," the young nun mutters, searching for words. She slices her fingers slowly across her neck. Her hands cup my cheeks, warm but unsteady. *"Mio cara amica—"*

*"Pardonatemi,"* a booming voice travels down the convent hall, the kind that makes you want to straighten up and take notice.

The two nuns do just that—in a snap. Behind them, a tall, elegant woman in a slightly different habit takes long strides toward us, narrowing her eyes at me. I have to assume she's the Mother Superior here, but she's nothing like the black-cloaked Darth Vader we had at my boarding school back in Cincinnati. Instead, she's an apparition in all white, just like an angel. Yet as she nears us, her crystalline blue eyes betray a hint of coldness, cruelty even. When her gaze meets mine, she shakes her head.

"I'm sorry, but my girls don't speak English very well," she says with a rolling Italian accent and a smile that could sell a thousand Cadillacs.

I take a step back, floored by this glossy version of nunhood who appears custom made for Venetian tourists. I can't help thinking that despite her formidable gaze, she's immensely profitable to the church somehow.

"You want to know where the hostel is?" she presses, eyeing our humble clothing and the last remnants of bread and cheese in my hand like I'm a vagabond. She sweeps her hand toward the magnificent hallway. "Or are you seeking luxury accommodations here at the convent?"

Though her words sound vaguely encouraging, I can tell from her stance that she's all blockade. Sleek, beautiful—and not about to let us enter unless we unload a ton of euros for the privilege.

Something tells me she knows we don't have a dime.

I steal a glance at Creek. But he isn't looking at me—he's scanning the interior of the convent like he's casing the joint. All work and swift deduction. Then his eyes scrutinize the tearful young nun as if for clues.

"I'm looking for Alessia de Bargona!" I blurt. I don't mean to be so damn loud, and I know tears are already welling in my eyes. I can't stop it—my emotions are totally raw, and the way that young nun said "Ali" with such hope in her voice made me feel like I'm on the right track.

But the Mother Superior bristles at the mere mention of Alessia's name. Her long nose scrunches for a moment as if that word were a profanity.

"You think you're the first *turistas* searching for *monaca pazzesca*? The crazy nun of Venice?" She sighs wistfully, thrusting her hands into her habit pockets. "Yes, she was famous in this *sestiere*. But that was a long time ago, and I'm afraid she's dead, *piccolina*. Suicide. Such tragedies are typical of her...kind. And sad, too, since you do look a little like her—"

She cups my cheek and stares into my eyes. Instantly, icy fingers shoot down my spine.

"Then the de Bargona family will know where she's buried, right?" Creek cuts in without missing a beat. Tall himself, he steps forward and towers over the Mother Superior to meet her gaze, flashing the coldest dagger-scar smile I've ever witnessed in my life. It's a smile that says *I don't believe you for two seconds, bitch*. It's a smile that says, *And I'm ready to snap you in two if you don't give me what I want*.

I watch the Mother Superior's throat tremble as she

swallows uncomfortably. Her cheeks stiffen in an effort to retain her composure, but when Creek forces the heavy door open wider and folds his arms impatiently—one might even say brutally—I can tell by her eyes that she's rattled.

"Th-there are no church burials for blasphemers," she insists, "crazy women with visions who hang themselves. To find her remains, you'll have to ask the de Bargonas."

She points toward a bend in the Grand Canal nearby, its waters glistening at dawn. "Their *palazzo* is well known in the —what do you call it?" She pats her arm. "*La Volta*—the elbow of Venice. Look for the *Rio di Ca' Bargona*. Their *palazzo* is there. Only they have the answers you seek."

"*Grazie!*" I reply way too loud, but it's no use. The second that word escapes my lips, the thick door slams in my face, clicking with the sound of a heavy lock, and Creek has to steady me on my feet to keep me from falling. But balance is the last of my worries right now. All I can think about is the haunted way that young nun looked at me. Piercing and full of loss, as if *I* might be her precious Ali.

And my mind races, wondering if it's true that my mother is really dead.

## ❧ 6 ❧

My foot slips on the curved, terra cotta roof tiles that are slick in the morning dew.

Normally, I'd have screamed my guts out by now, but Creek grabs me before I can slide to my death on a Venetian street below.

"I've got you," he whispers, his strong arms righting me so I can take a breath.

I fold my head against his chest to clear the dizziness for a second and refuse to look down. His heart pumps hard against his flannel shirt to meet my cheek.

We're skittering along the rooftops like loose cats.

Crazy?

You bet.

But as Creek told me after the convent, this is the safest way to reach the de Bargona's ancestral home. "Most thugs are stupid—they don't bother to look up," he said. So instead of slipping through alleys as the sun begins to rise, we're hopping from roof to roof, navigating the sea of tiles that make up the interconnected puzzle of this city. I thank God for the occasional sculpted chimney that I can cling to for dear life to regain my balance.

"How do you like being a fugitive again?" Creek smiles wickedly, displaying that infernal scar. He shows off this time by making a grand leap to a flatter roof between two palazzos and skipping over the tiles like a sprite. My heart jumps in my chest, but I'm not about to give myself away. I throw out my arms like wings.

"Fine!" I reply, vaulting to the roof to do an elegant twirl, just to see his eyes grow wide. "In fact, I find it rather liberating." Wow, those ten years of forced ballet lessons finally seemed to pay off.

And in more ways than I suspected—

Because the way Creek looks at me right now, as I do another pirouette to show off like he did, makes all my defenses crumble. He stares at me as though I'm a rare and graceful bird, one he'd give anything to call his own. The early sunlight glints off his hair, making it shine as bright as the gold crosses that dot the city, and I see him stand a little taller. With a gallant gesture, he holds out his hand as if calling my heart to give flight and alight upon his arm.

Just then, I see a blue bird glide by.

It's much bigger than the usual songbirds we used to see in the forest around Bender Lake. As it makes its course toward the de Bargona's *palazzo*, a blue feather floats down on the tiles between us.

Usually this wouldn't disturb me. Except I couldn't help

noticing that the bird has red legs—just like the one Granny Tinker whittled.

As it flaps its wings, inexplicably, it perches on Creek's arm and gives a hoarse cry reminiscent of a falcon. Just as quickly as it landed, it moves on in the direction of the rising sun.

And I have goose bumps all over my body.

Creek meets me halfway, picking up the feather like a souvenir.

"One more roof, sweetheart," he says, and I feel the lump rise in my throat.

How on earth am I supposed to introduce myself to the de Bargonas?

Just ring their doorbell and say, "Hi! Remember me? The bastard child you ditched? Well I'm baaaaack—"

"You're not going to say a word," Creek advises. He strides toward me and gently grips my shoulders, then traces the blue feather along my cheek for reassurance.

God, he can be spooky sometimes!

With the way he senses my thoughts, part of me wonders if he's a distant relative of Granny Tinker, too. Or perhaps, because of his rough childhood, he's simply had a lifetime of ferreting out people's motives.

Creek wraps his arm around me protectively and points in the direction of the de Bargona's home with the feather.

"Listen, Robin—we're simply going to knock on the de Bargona's door and act like tourists asking about whatever happened to that crazy nun of Venice. I'm pretty sure they'll have a pat answer meant to deflect curiosity seekers, and we'll take it from there."

I nod and feel Creek's arm cinch around me tighter, as

though he can feel my heightening anxiety over whether the de Bargonas will recognize me. He turns to face me, his blue eyes reflecting the amber sheen of the morning light.

"Of course they're gonna recognize you," he says flatly, as though that's as obvious as the weather. "Everyone says you look like Alessia. But while you're busy pretending to be a dumbshit American who'll buy any story they dish out, I'll 'accidentally' scrape my hand on something and then head to the bathroom rather than bleed on their precious floor. At which time I'll case the joint for files and clues of what really happened to your mom. All you gotta do is keep fluttering your hands and asking them silly questions about their house and furniture till I return and give the go ahead to get the hell out of there. Sound like a plan?"

I'm already chewing my lip on the possibilities. And naturally, I want to nod my head at the typical genius of Creek's strategy.

But I'm too overwhelmed by the ethereal beauty of the morning rays that have already begun to swallow Creek's body in gold.

And also by the knowledge that, on this red tile roof at dawn, this could well be the last morning we'll ever be so carefree.

The two of us—we're both perched on this steep rooftop of adulthood as we overlook the misty morning of Venice. From here on out, every choice we make matters.

I heave a sigh, knowing that my search for my mom is likely to tear a hole straight through my heart. This last moment of not knowing the truth about her is a luxury, not unlike the lovely vista we have before us. After today, I'll never have the same innocence again, or be able to conjure up pretty fantasies about her. Our mother-daughter story, for good or bad, will be all too clear. And Creek and I will just have to go forward with what we've learned.

But one thing I know for certain: At this moment, I'm standing beside the most beautiful, sun-drenched man-boy I've ever seen in my life. And like always, Creek does the very thing that terrifies me most—

He releases his grip and dashes across the terra cotta rooftop to make a flying leap, spread-eagled and laughing, and lands on the de Bargona's *palazzo.*

"You coming, Robin?" He swivels around and extends his arms wide, inviting me with his most sparkling smile. The tail of his flannel shirt flaps gently in the breeze.

God help me—how can I resist a future like that?

Feeling mischievous, I dip a curtsy to the morning sun and do my very best *fouetté* ballet maneuver, just to taunt fate, and then nod.

"Ready to fly!" I cry, keeping my eyes focused on Creek. With a quick shake of my head to dispel any remaining fears, I charge across the rooftop and hurl my body into thin air.

"The first morning tour begins in ten minutes," a woman announces in a clipped British accent. I glance at Creek, floored by the cluster of tourists who've already beat us to the de Bargona's door. Creek guides my body to disappear inside the huddle so no gunmen can spot us easily from the street.

"Please stay outside the lobby until we get an accurate head count."

Thinking fast, Creek grabs a few tickets that have fallen on the stoop from past tours and casually hands them to our apparent docent. She's too flustered by the eagerness of the crowd to notice the crumpled tickets, as well as distracted by the miles of fabric she has to maneuver in the brocade gown she's wearing, similar to what I imagine Venetian women donned during the Renaissance. Beside her is another tour guide in an ornate dress who repeats everything she says in Italian, and afterwards gazes at her cell phone to check the time, yawning as though wishing this was over and she could get more espresso. My lips curl in a smirk at the weird anachronism, until Creek sends me a stern look.

"Concentrate," he whispers. "And don't make yourself noticeable."

I lift two fingers in salute, just to bug him. "Aye, Sarge," I whisper, but Creek doesn't give me a second glance. He's carefully monitoring every face who's braved the cold doorstep of the de Bargona's *palazzo* to make sure we're not under any threat. As the grand door of the mansion opens wide, the crush of tourists surges forward, and I hear the jingle of euros changing hands and beep of credit card machines taking money. All this makes me wonder: How rich can the de Bargonas really be if they have to loan out their home for tours?

But my curiosity is cut short by the shock of what I spy on the wall—

It's *me.*

Wearing a crimson gown in an oil portrait with a glistening ruby heart on a chain around my neck.

In the painting, my eyes look enraged and my hair collects around the ruby in wild, dark tendrils. Dangling from one ear flashes a gold gypsy earring.

The stone in my back pocket leaps angrily.

And just about burns my ass.

"Excuse me," I pipe up to the English-speaking tour guide, "do you happen to have a tissue?"

She points to a box of Kleenex on the money-changing table and I head over and grab a handful, stuffing them into my pocket before my butt develops blisters. Creek shoots me a look that could kill for drawing attention to myself. I point to my pocket, hoping he'll get it. Still, he folds his arms unhappily and hints at me to blend back into the crowd with his eyes.

"Behold Martiya de Bargona!" the tour guide cries out, flipping on a floodlight that shines on the oil painting in a gilded frame. "The most beautiful woman to grace Italy's Renaissance."

All at once the lobby becomes hushed.

"That's who you've come to hear about today, right? Either that or the crazy nun of Venice?"

A few chuckles erupt from the crowd as the other tour guide echoes her words in Italian.

Meanwhile, the English docent walks beneath the portrait and picks up a jewel-encrusted cross from a table. She holds it up as if casting a blessing or exorcising an evil spirit—I can't tell which.

"Martiya de Bargona and the crazy nun are known in this *sestiere* as the Devil and Angel of Venice. Believe it or not, though centuries apart, these two women's lives were quite intertwined. By the way, how many of you would like your fortunes told today?"

Several tourists sheepishly raise their hands, but not me—mine's locked to my side so I won't make a spectacle of myself and annoy Creek.

"Well, fortunes are what the de Bargona's history is really about. And it all begins with blood…"

I feel a chill rattle down my spine, considering the wound I carved into Creek's arm two days ago that's barely begun to heal, and the rich way his blood tasted on my lips. The stone lurches again in my pocket, and I shift my weight to ignore it.

"I'm not sure how many of you would be brave enough to try this," the tour guide continues, her gown swishing as she strides back toward the crowd, "but legend has it that Martiya de Bargona was once the best gypsy fortune teller in all of Italy. So effective at informing others how to make a profit, in fact, that Nicolo de Bargona, a mildly successful merchant in Venice at the time, gave her father an entire sack of gold with only one hitch. He demanded Martiya's hand in marriage."

She sets down the cross and holds up an antique hat pin to her palm.

"Anyone like to prick a little blood?"

The crowd murmurs uneasily.

"Because that was Martiya's fortune-telling stock in trade. She would prick your hand and then smear the blood on your palm to see your life and love lines better. Unfortunately, her magical powers only secured her tragic fate as old man Nicolo de Bargona's unwilling, sixteen-year-old bride." The docent sighs. "You see, Martiya's father was so besotted by the sight of all that gold that he forced his young daughter into an arranged marriage—and to leave the love of her life, the dashingly handsome gypsy boy Bohemas."

What was once a chill down my back has now become a fire that consumes my body. Nervously, I glance around to see if my clothes might have erupted into flames. But it's the stone —Martiya—emanating so much angry heat that it's making me sweat in places I didn't know I had.

"What, um, became of her?" a meek woman in a touristy sweatshirt inquires, wringing her hands as if the answer might determine the fate of true love for us all.

The tour guide shakes her head. "Ah, that poor devil Martiya. She was furious at her father for trading her to a merchant. Out of revenge, she stole her father's priceless ruby —the very Heart of the Gypsies—that legend claims brings riches wherever it goes. It was supposed to have originated with a Sultan in India, but along with prosperity it brings a terrible curse. Whoever steals it renders its former owner impoverished—so Martiya's gypsy father and his band were forced to roam in rags throughout Europe from then on. But the bearer of the Heart of the Gypsies can never find true love until the stone is returned. Martiya was willful and thought she could beat this fate, and she kept sneaking out at night for clandestine meetings with her old flame Bohemas. But years later, Nicolo de Bargona found them in a forest outside of Venice during Mardi Gras and killed them both. Could that have been the curse at work? No one knows for sure. But history claims Martiya laughed in Nicolo's face and tasted her lover's blood right before she died, catapulting her magical powers to that of *Thagarni*, or the Gypsy Queen. She became a soul thief—one who could absorb the pain of all those who are broken hearted—as long as they join her spirit inside the ruby heart."

A collective gasp surfaces from the crowd.

"Where's the stone now?" asks a portly tourist who looks at the painting as if he's fallen for Martiya and her charms.

The docent glances aside, then sets the hat pin on the cross and clasps her hands. "Sadly," she replies, "it was lost—or perhaps stolen—about eighteen years ago, when the family went to America on business. Since that time, the de Bargona pasta sauce company stock has fallen dramatically. They once used to brag that their marinara ran in a river of blood from Venice to the rest of the world. But now, like many companies in the recession, business has become quite challenging."

And that's when I lose my breath—

Because it's all starting to make sense to me. Ever since Alessia slipped my dad the stone, his fortunes began to soar. And now the de Bargona's appear so broke that they're forced to give tours of their former grandeur.

Before I finish the thought, Creek gives me a nudge and eyes me with understanding.

"What about the famous Angel of Venice?" asks a dreamy-looking woman with long blonde hair with ribbons in it. "How does the crazy nun's story coincide with—"

"There is *no* Angel of Venice," a deep-throated Italian voice cuts her off.

The English tour guide startles as a distinguished gentleman descends a staircase to the lobby where we stand. He has grey, finely-groomed hair and is wearing an elegant silk suit the color of steel. His dark eyes appear severe.

"C-Conté de Bargona!" the tour guide stammers. "I-I didn't know you were in residence today—"

The man holds up a hand to halt her chatter like the pope.

And I notice he refuses to glance up. In fact, everything about his being seems to mentally shut her out along with the portrait of Martiya above us, as though he believes them to be beneath him. He stares with a cold, level gaze across the lobby at the crowd.

"*Sì*, it may be true that my daughter looked a little like her ancestor Martiya," he concedes in a rich Italian lilt. "But I'm afraid she died in a *tragico*—how do you call it?—accident, years ago. She was a good nun, blessed with visions of *angelos*. So there's no *scandalo* here."

His bottomless dark eyes scan the cluster of tourists and lock on mine, freezing my heart in place, as though he'd expected to find me here. His stare is so arresting that I half-believe I'll see a line of frost between us, and I actually seek to palm the stone in my pocket for warmth. I huddle closer to Creek for protection.

"Now, won't you sample some our world famous marinara?" he commands more than requests. "Step left to the *cucina* where you can try our latest varieties."

Like a herd of obedient circus elephants, the crowd heads one by one to the kitchen. He gives them a smile, but oddly, I've never felt colder in my life. De Bargona's presence feels like a dark shadow across my soul that mysteriously manages to steal heat.

Even the stone in my pocket seems to cool against my jeans.

And despite the shuffling noise of the tourists heading to the kitchen, I hear a voice whisper in my ear.

*Kill him! Don't miss your chance—kill him NOW...*

To my surprise, Creek steps toward a wall and grabs the edge of a sword hanging beside a tapestry. My hands rise to stifle my scream. He couldn't possibly have heard the same voice, could he—

But rather than a hasty murder, Creek slices his palm along the edge of the sword out of fake curiosity, ripping open his flesh. He fans his fingers to allow the blood to drip to the alabaster floor.

"Fuck!" He cries like it was a mistake, spreading his boots wide. A crimson puddle collects between his feet.

The Italian tour guide flutters around him, all jerking hand gestures and staccato words that sound like curses. *"Bagno! Bagno!"* She orders, pointing up the staircase and handing him tissues to stop the bleeding. Before Creek dashes up the steps, he winks at me, and I thank my lucky stars that the Conté de Bargona doesn't appear to notice our connection. He's too busy in the kitchen, opening up jars of sauce and proudly ladeling his product over pasta that's been prepared for the tourists. Yet the chill of his presence still hovers over me like an unwanted cloak. As I give Creek a swift nod and head toward the kitchen, I feel a tap on my shoulder.

Swiveling around, I half-expect to see the Italian docent with a few swear words for me, too—and ready to hand me a mop. But I find myself gazing at a man so desperately handsome he steals all breath from my chest.

His dark unruly hair frames his cheekbones in random curls, and his face is all hard angles—smooth and sharp as

Venetian cut glass. Eyes twinkling, he gives me a broad smile filled with enough charm to send a dozen girls' hearts into spirals. The second that thought strikes me, a strange flutter arises in my gut and works its way out to my limbs in waves. I feel the stone throb against my pocket, harassing me with whispers that are drowned out by the pulsing sound of blood rushing to my brain.

Because something about this man's eyes mystify me and holds me into place. Although he appears in his early 20s at best, somehow there's a shadow in his gaze that bears the weight of a very old man. Like the other tour guides, he's dressed in period clothing from the Renaissance, an ivory peasant shirt and pants with brocade detail and black boots. I have to presume he's here to help with the tour.

"You want to see the rest of the *palazzo, sì mia amica?*"

He doesn't wait for an answer, holding out his arm in an oddly cavalier way, as though he were about to ask me to dance at a ball. "Here, let me show you the map room. The group will-a join us soon."

I hesitate, grinding my heels into the alabaster floor.

Truth be told, I'd love some of that pasta in the kitchen because I'm still starving, even after the bread and cheese we wolfed down from the nun's handout earlier. But as I hear the Conté de Bargona bragging about his blood-red sauce, I can't help thinking anything's better than being near him right now. He *did* seem to recognize me—at least as someone who looks spooky-close to his ancestor. Does that mean he pegs me as his daughter's bastard child?

Before I can entertain the possibilities, the tour guide forcefully whisks me up several stairs by the time I manage to jerk my elbow away from him. Glancing over my shoulder, I spot the other docents cleaning up the blood spill, and I wonder how Creek is doing with rifling through desks and files. At least this trip to the map room could buy us some more time. I give the young man a hint of smile.

He responds by breaking free of my arm and bolting up the steps to the landing, where I can see a room at the top covered in yellowed, archaic maps. Flashing that broad smile again, he disappears, and all of a sudden the landing is filled with a warm, inviting glow. Curious, I head to the map room and find him standing beside two French doors that are opened wide to a balcony.

"The only way to truly know *Venezia* is by its light," he says with a certain triumph in his voice.

He's merely a silhouette now, his amazing physique backlit by the subtle morning sunshine, almost like a phantom.

As my eyes readjust to the outline of his dark contours, I notice there are Mardi Gras masks hanging on the walls next to the double doors. Their hollow, black eyes and faces empty of the warmth of human flesh spook me a little.

"A-Aren't we here to see the maps?" I remind him, cautious about stepping any further into this room. I turn slightly to glance into the hallway, my eyes hunting past several doors that have been left ajar.

"Creek," I whisper sharply. "Where are you…"

No answer.

Dammit—

Returning my gaze to my host, I find he's grabbed two of the masks and he's motioning for me to step out onto the balcony.

"Maps only record the past," he insists. "Come, let's see the future."

I draw in a breath, rationalizing it won't hurt to stall for more time. "OKAY," I voice too loudly, hoping it might help Creek detect where I am, "I CAN CHECK OUT THE VIEW WITH YOU FOR A MINUTE."

Not a sound stirs from the hallway.

Only my echo as it slowly fades away.

With a sigh, and several excuses in mind to bolt free from this guy as soon as I hear evidence of Creek, I shrug my shoulders and stroll out to the balcony to take in the sights.

Before us is the Grand Canal, its waters a deep murky green with hints of shimmer from the early sun that's begun to peek above the elegant domes and spires. A layer of mist still shrouds the city like a blanket, making it appear hazy and sepia toned, and every bit as ancient as its architecture belies.

"Tell me," the young man asks, "what do you see, Rubina?"

My heart skips a beat.

I haven't told him my name yet. Much less the Italian version the de Bargonas gave me at birth—

And I feel the ruby wobble to match my quickening pulse.

"Um, I see green water," I pipe up, extremely antsy now to get back to Creek. The time for politeness is way over, and as I spin on my heels to go inside, his hand stops my shoulder with the abruptness of stone. He holds up a glittering gold mask.

"*Un momento.* Just put it on—then tell me what you see."

He adjusts a shiny black mask over his face that instantly makes him look foreboding.

"This will only take a second," his accent rolls in an almost musical tone, "I promise. I simply want you to understand. Everything in *Venezia* changes. The light, the masks, the people —nothing is ever as it seems."

Annoyed, I slip the gold mask over my head, only because I calculate Creek will emerge from the hallway any second now. Interestingly, when I glance back over the canal, the water has transformed from emerald to an ethereal amethyst with hints of rose that sparkle over the currents as the sun ascends more boldly over the city. It's beautiful—there's no doubt about it. But it's way past time for me to join Creek.

Just as I open my mouth to say a swift goodbye, the man grabs my face in his hands and swallows me in a kiss.

Not just any kiss—

He wraps himself around me as though he could pour his spirit like a searing liquid into my throbbing veins.

And the fluttering I felt earlier now runs up and down my spine like wildfire, stinging me with a heat that focuses like a laser on the stone inside my pocket.

It takes every ounce of strength I have to break free from him. And the second I do, I haul off and slap him so hard it knocks that black mask off his face.

"WHAT THE FUCK ARE YOU DOING!" I cry, reeling, my fists clenched tight.

Out of the corner of my eye, I spy a wash of red. The bold sun now glows like an angry ball that pierces the mist of the city, coating the entire canal the color of blood.

The young man gazes at me without apology.

"I only wanted to kiss something beautiful before it dies," he says. "Because make no mistake—Vittorio de Bargona will kill you."

He steals another kiss before I can gather the wherewithal to shove his ass back.

"Go to the gypsies, Rubina," he whispers, "out in the countryside. That is, if you want to *live*."

In that moment, he becomes hazy, like the mist that still threads between the buildings of the city. Then he disappears.

And all that's left at my feet is his shiny black mask.

## 7

"**G**o—go!" Creek cries as a bullet whistles over our heads. It's been shot with a silencer, but that doesn't get rid of its eerie, high-pitched wail. Creek's running toward me in a flash with a tattered envelope in his hand. Before I can ask questions, he's engulfed my body in his arms and leaped over the wrought-iron bars of the balcony.

This isn't exactly how I imagined being carried over a threshold by the love of my life...

Straight into a baptism of sea water.

We are falling, falling toward the deep canal that shines crimson on the surface, until we splash and are swallowed by its murky liquid.

All churning arms and legs, our breaths rise in bubbles around us. I can see bullets piercing straight lines through water, each one making a sharp blooping sound, until Creek grabs me by the arm and drags me to where the canal is darkened by shadows. My lungs are about to burst, yet I know we can't surface for air until we're out of gunshot range.

And there's hardly a question who wants me dead now.

But I've got no time for deciphering intrigue—my chest feels like it's burning as I follow Creek beneath a pier that juts out over the canal. Just as we pass the dark, water-soaked pillars, a hand grabs my shirt.

And lifts me up!

I'm gasping and pedaling my feet, cursing and taking swings in air, unable to see who's got me by the collar.

When my body is unceremoniously dumped into the bed of a gondola and covered by a royal blue blanket.

Before I can blink, Creek joins me, wet as a fish.

He's heaving for breath and spitting out salt water. I half expect him to rise up swinging, like I did, but instead he clasps his hand over my mouth and pulls the blanket over both of us to blot out the sun.

It's totally dark now. I know my eyes must be as large as saucers as I feel the gondola sway in a slow, leisurely glide across the canal, as though we're merely tourists starting our day. And I hear a dreamy alto voice soar over our heads.

*Che bella cosa è na jurnata 'e sole,*
*n'aria serena dopo na tempesta.*
*Pe' ll'aria fresca para già na festa…*

I have no idea who's singing or what the words mean. And I couldn't be more confused as Creek wrestles me into a hug like we're two vacationers getting way too frisky with each other. I'm about to ask questions when I feel Creek's hand stroke a dripping wet lock from my forehead.

"Shhh…he's helping us," Creek whispers. "Work with me."

"Who?" I reply, unable to imagine why anyone would stow away a couple of damp foreigners—who're getting *shot at*, no less.

"The gondolier who first brought us here," Creek says, pressing his finger to my lips. We can hear angry shouts in Italian from where the de Bargona's home must be, but fortunately they grow quieter in the distance and disappear.

I snuggle up to Creek, who brushes his lips sweetly against mine as if he were simply swiping a kiss between dances at my old boarding school. But the truth—that makes me want to hyperventilate right now—is that we've once again barely escaped with our lives.

"Creek," I whisper in a shaky voice, feeling goose bumps spread across my body, made only worse by my wet clothes, "why on earth would this guy help us?"

I feel Creek's chest hesitate, then rise and fall again slowly, with that same caution he always shows before he decides whether to mention something he thinks is too dark for me to know.

But I *want* to know.

I elbow him until he relents.

"He's…helping us…," Creek pauses, "because you're not the only one the de Bargonas have tried to kill, baby. You heard the tour guide—she likened them to a 'river of blood'. And something tells me pasta sauce ain't the only thing she's talking about."

He rubs my arms to ward away the shivers.

"Your grandfather, the Count, has the coldest eyes I've ever seen in my life, Robin—even among members of the mob. A guy like that won't think twice about making people...disappear."

My trembling comes in waves now, despite my efforts to will it to stop so I can seem tough to Creek. I pull the blanket tighter around myself, hoping our gondolier is still steering us in shadows. "C-Creek," I press, not wanting to have any delusions about this trip, "somehow, he must've gotten tipped off that I came to Italy and that I've got the stone. D-do you think we're really going to die?"

He is quiet for a long time. And part of me can't help wondering if this gondola will become our coffin, no matter who helps us or how hard we try. Surely de Bargona's henchmen will track us down as our boat glides through the mists of this old city.

But then Creek rolls gently on top of me, sliding his hands up and down my shoulders, hips and thighs, attempting to warm me with his whole being. I feel his breath alight on my cheeks and then my neck, like a sweet and defiant reminder that we're alive and still breathing. He sweeps back the sopping hair from my eyes that I hope hide my welling tears, but that I don't think fool him for a minute.

"Not if I have anything to do with it, sweetheart," he replies.

Our path is a bramble.

And that's the point—

Our kindly gondolier calls it a "gypsy trail", these miles and miles of dense thickets flanked by trees that meander around fields in northern Italy's countryside.

When I look really close, I can trace the narrow path which winds its way along creeks and draws, hidden from nearby roads and villages. It seems like a secret route used only by outlaws and maybe their horses who're on the run. Just like us.

If I didn't know better, I'd say we're right back in the boondocks by Bender Lake—a notorious shelter for those who want to disappear. And as I glance at Creek, and his ease at navigating this nearly impossible wall of shrubs and trees that appear rarely touched by man, that thought comforts me a little.

Our gondolier is acting as our guide for only a bit longer before he returns to work. As he walks, he nudges me and points to markers on old fences and stumps, muttering things in Italian. I don't understand him, but it's clear that these carvings have a pattern—a skull and crossbones means the water isn't good, a stick figure with a badge indicates watch out for police. Then there are drawings of grapes and orchard trees, which I assume point to a good spot to steal fruit. But the one that scares me is an outline of the Grim Reaper. Was somebody killed here? Or are the farmers merely unwelcoming? I'm too afraid to ask.

The sun is high now, and its heat warms the leftover dew on the ground, making our path humid and sticky as hell. Fanning my damp shirt, I keep wondering when this hike will end. It feels like it's been hours already, and I finally muster up the guts to tap our guide on the shoulder.

"How much farther?" I ask, panting but trying to make my voice sound grateful.

He stops and points at the sun, drawing down his arm level with the horizon before he pauses. "You will know."

The way he looks into my eyes sends tingles down my spine.

It isn't worry.

And it isn't even fatigue.

It's...reverence?

To my astonishment, he takes my hand and gives it a kiss, then holds it tenderly to his cheek as though I'm his very own daughter. His skin is warm, and his touch makes the stone tremble in my pocket.

*"Benedizioni, Thagarni,"* he says with a wistful smile.

And turns around to leave.

Creek wraps his arm around my shoulder and holds me still.

"Let him go," he urges, sensing my nerves about proceeding without a guide. It makes me feel like we're lost without a compass, in search of a strange gypsy band we don't even know. Will they really offer us protection—can I believe the promise of a creepy ghost who looked eerily like some guy in my vision? I never mentioned it to a soul, not even to Creek. But the gondolier seems to think so, because his plan was to walk us halfway to what he called the *cherchie zingari*, a caravan of gypsies who are known to harbor fugitives.

"That man's done enough for us already," Creek points

out, giving me a squeeze. "He wouldn't have brought us this far if he didn't think we'd make it okay."

I nod, knowing it's true. But when I glance back, just to call out a *grazie* to the guy before he disappears into the thicket, I realize there's no one there.

Nothing but a gold gypsy earring that lies on a bed of leaves on our path, sparkling in a patch of sun.

Had it been there before, and I simply didn't notice?

Just then, a warm breeze caresses my cheek and gently swirls around me like a protective spirit. As it fades away, I spot a blue-gray bird that alights upon an old, rotting fence post nearby.

*You will know*, I hear a low voice hover between us like a mist.

The blue bird leans back its head and releases a raspy cry. Then it lifts its wide wings and takes flight, heading north and vanishing from our sight.

## 8

"Creek," I manage to sputter, breathless, "am I going nuts, or are we being haunted?"

We've managed to climb a steep hill and it's nearly dark, but ever since we left the gondolier my mind's been a swirl. It doesn't help matters that all around us the trees have started to look black and gothic like something from an old horror movie. Any second, I expect one to reach out and grab us. But like usual, Creek is totally in his element in nature, calm and cool as the granite boulders that have begun to crop up on the hillsides. Near as I can tell, we've reached a rolling stretch of vineyards that back up against the blue outline of a mountain range at dusk. Every once in a while, I pluck a few raisins leftover from last year's grape harvest that didn't make the cut. They taste insanely sweet on my tongue— a sure sign that I'm exhausted and we haven't eaten for hours.

Creek stops for a moment and gazes at the sunset that

bleeds through the trees. He seems unfazed by the hunger he must be feeling and ignores my small handout of raisins.

"To answer your question," he sighs, keeping his focus on the red-gold color in the west, "You're nutty as a fucking loon."

He turns and gives me that lop-sided smile that always makes my heart soar.

"But here's the thing about loons," he threads his fingers over my head and gently through my wild, curly hair. "They're highly sensitive creatures. Granny Tinker nicknames them the ghosts of the lake, with the way their calls echo across the water and haunt the air when they're hidden in the mist. Whenever you hear a loon, she says, make a wish, because your dream will soon come true."

He brushes his lips past my temple and cups his hand to my ear. Then he makes the softest, loneliest bird call I've ever heard, like the voice of someone mournful hailing from beyond the grave.

"Don't blame the spirits for reaching out to you, Robin," he whispers in that low, smoky voice of his that sends my nerve endings on fire. "They're just lonely—and you are very, very beautiful."

With that, his lips press against mine, his palms cradling my jaw as though he were drinking from a cup, long and slow. Then his hand reaches to the small of my back, and he arches me over his arm and tenderly lays me down on the forest floor.

As hungry as I am, the rest of my body is starved for so much more—

I want to rip his clothes off this minute, be free and naked in this wild bramble as if we'd somehow stumbled upon Eden. Yet even though I can feel Creek's every muscle snap at my touch, reaching for the warmth of my fingers, his hand stops mine from quickly unraveling every button and zipper on his frame.

"Robin," he gasps, startled, "do you see them?"

For a moment I wonder if he means more ghosts.

I shake my head, confused.

He peers through the branches, pointing to a small cluster of trees on the horizon.

With the sun behind them, I can make out the dark outline of some people who look like they're setting up a camp in the woods, with the silhouette of tents and wagons on either side. Tethered to their vehicles are several horses.

"It's them," Creek's lip curls into a half-smile. He reaches over and plucks the gold earring from its bed of leaves, tossing and catching it in air. "The gypsies."

"But how do we know if they'll help us like the gondolier did?" I ask, daunted by their shadowy presence. "Or if they're even for *real*."

My own words make me shudder. Uneasy, I strip a few leaves from my hair.

At that moment, the wind sends a strange scuffling sound like whispers.

Creek pulls the blue feather he'd saved from his pocket and runs it along my cheek with a thoughtful glance. "That's the thing, we don't know," he replies, swiping another kiss. "We'll never know. We'll have to wing it, like usual."

He's so handsome in the thin sunlight that filters through

the trees, caressing his rugged face and tousled hair with hints of amber warmth. My body's aching for us to be skin on skin, with nothing between us but heat. I half expect to die from the rush of blood between my thighs, working its way up and making me feel as if my insides are on fire. Creek smiles and leans against me, hard against my pelvis, and the look in his eyes is all yearning, all...*possession*. Yet at the same time, his expression has that familiar, endless sadness, as though forever haunted at the edges by...loss.

I swallow a ragged breath, knowing every woman he's ever tried to love has either died or deserted him.

But that doesn't fucking mean *me*.

I force up my chin.

I've staked a claim to his heart and I'm here to stay—and with all my might, I try to let my eyes burn that message into his. To make him feel it coming from my body and soul in waves.

Creek doesn't look away. But he doesn't exactly fall into my embrace either.

Chewing on the inside of my cheek, I roll up his flannel shirt sleeve to remind him of the scar that must still be painful on his arm.

"Partners," I say adamantly, tracing the letters of the word with my finger and watching him hold back his flinch. "We're always gonna be partners, Creek, 'cause you couldn't get rid of me if you tried."

Impulsively, I hold up my hand to show Creek the stain of his own blood on my fingertip. With a devil-may-care smirk, I wave it in front of him like I'd dipped my finger in a sweet berry liqueur and brazenly take a lick. Fuck Martiya and all her weird plans—if this act binds my soul to Creek's forever, so be it.

I totally expect the ruby to wobble in my pocket and throw off sparks, whispering bizarre demands until it practically sizzles my ass.

But instead, it remains still.

Out of the corner of my eye, I spy the silhouettes of the gypsies seated around their camp in the distance with a small bonfire in front of them. One by one, they each turn to face me and stand up.

As we walk hesitantly up to the camp at twilight, the gypsies stare me down, almost unblinking, with a strange look of wonder as if I were a long-lost cousin who'd run off to find her fortune in childhood, now returned years later like a ghost. The light of their bonfire warms their faces, and at first, only the men approach me with folded arms, jabbering in their gypsy tongue and peering cautiously at Creek as if he might be dangerous.

They're right, I nod to myself. He *is*.

But when one of them pulls out a knife—or is that a machete?—with a shiny steel blade as long my forearm, I instinctively hold out my hand before Creek can intervene.

And they all take a step back.

I swear, I thought I saw the biggest guy among them tremble.

What the fuck? I feel as if I could slice my arm in the air

and they'd part like the Red Sea. Do they think I possess some kind of magical powers?

Strangely enough, Creek remains motionless and silent at my side, flanking me as close as a shadow. Yet I can feel the tension rising in him as he scans the small group, his mind tallying precisely what it would require to kill each one of them if they get anywhere near me.

So much for taking refuge among the gypsies.

I draw in a deep breath, feeling lied to by a bunch of capricious ghosts. These people look like they want to kill me —not exactly like they're ready to hide us or hand us a bowl of the stew they're cooking over their campfire.

"I'm looking for my mother," I blurt out, troubled by their response and hoping to all hell they might understand a little English.

And that's when she approaches as softly as a night breeze. I feel her before I see her, this woman who slinks up like a cat from behind me in the fading daylight. She is all darkness—a tangle of sable hair that threads over ink eyes, wearing a ruffled maroon blouse and a dusky riding coat that cinches at her waist and fans out at her hips, extending all the way to her ankles with a slit up the back as if she were about to ride sidesaddle. If I didn't know better, I'd peg her as Catherine, that wild and tempestuous creature from *Wuthering Heights*—the last novel I was forced to read before bolting from my old high school for good.

Creek eyes the woman fiercely, as if she might have a dagger up her sleeve. And there's no doubt in my mind he's already planned how to break her neck.

But she doesn't look at him.

She doesn't even look at *me*.

Though we stand shoulder to shoulder, her gaze is steady upon the flames of the campfire that make her dark eyes and caramel skin glow.

"Your mother," her voice sounds deep and lush, like the throbbing of an old song, "she's already here, *shebari*."

At that moment, the fire crackles and snaps, flickering as red as the ruby in my pocket.

And my heart leaps with the flames.

Oh God, is she playing me? I wonder. I reach out to grab Creek's hand for strength and he squeezes it, knowing full well how desperately I want to find my mother. But then his grip tightens and holds me firm, as if to say *Don't believe everything you hear. After all, they're gypsies.*

"Come," the woman says, waving us toward the campfire. "You need food and rest." She points to a black pot—a cauldron, really—that's boiling with a heavenly-scented stew.

Though gentle, her words make the men fall away from us like attack dogs that've been warned to back down.

Except for Creek.

Like a wolf, his eyes track my every move, allowing me to follow her to the black pot before he steps into the tree shadows just beyond the fire's range, glaring at each of the gypsies in spite of his hunger.

But I can't stop myself. When the woman dishes some stew into a wooden bowl, I yank it from her hands like a feral child and spoon it into my mouth in large gulps.

It's *crazy* good!

Hunks of tender lamb and potatoes spiced with paprika and herbs that's so over-the-top delicious I pray it doesn't possess some magical spell. I feel selfish devouring it in front of Creek. Quickly, I spoon several more helpings from the pot back into the bowl and step beyond the fire ring to hand it to him.

When I turn around, the gypsies are gone—

All but the mysterious woman who served me stew.

"No-no," she waves her hand with a wry smile, as if reading my mind. "No *mulani*. There are no ghosts here." In the campfire's glow, two of her front teeth shine gold. "We are a welcoming people. But we need time to…how do you call it? Make friends. You watch—tomorrow they will sing you songs and tell stories. You won't be able to shut them up."

"Where's my mother?" I demand with a hiss, my fists clenched. Creek sets down his bowl and grips my shoulders so I can't dash toward her and take a swing.

Jesus Christ—add a little food to my belly and I become a bitch! My own violence unnerves me, but at this point I don't give a fuck about her gypsy pals or anything else on Italian soil. After being haunted and shot at *twice* in this god-forsaken country, all I want is to find my mother and get the hell out of here.

The woman crouches down on her heels and feels the ground for a stick, then pokes the fire, releasing a shower of sparks into the night air that look like stars.

She rests her elbows on her knees, quietly staring at the fire as if searching its orange and yellow and crimson hues like a crystal ball. God as my witness, for a second I thought I saw an image of my own face in the flames, swallowed by a sudden burst of red heat. When the woman lifts her gaze to us again, she appears to stare beyond me to where the last bloody inch of sun is slipping behind the horizon.

"*Dili pisliskurja,* the woman mutters softly with a sigh. "Don't you understand? Your mother is in your back pocket."

She throws her stick into the fire and rises to her feet.

"Now it's time to go to sleep."

## 9

I toss and turn on the downy blankets that remind me of Granny Tinker's old quilts, my eyes squinting at the rising sun.

Did that strange woman last night mean my "mother"—as in, my "ancestor"—is in my back pocket? The renowned Martiya? Or is she trying to tell me my mom's dead, like all the rumors claim, and her soul departed into the stone, too?

Anxious, I wriggle the ruby heart from my jeans and hold it in my palm.

Creek showed me the ragged letter he'd stolen from the de Bargonas while we were on the trail yesterday. With my heart in my throat, I'd unfolded the damp, yellowed page from the envelope—it was simply addressed to the de Bargonas eighteen years ago and had Alessia's name printed in the middle with these words:

*Istituto Mentale: montagne.*

Mental Institution…mountains.

Even I could figure out that much in Italian.

The message seemed cryptic, as if the family didn't want any more details about their daughter. And it was a long time ago. The "crazy nun of Venice" who used to see angels could have passed away, or killed herself, by now.

I glance at Creek lying beside me. We're nestled on a bed of blankets that the gypsies gave us in the small woods beside their camp. It's dawn and I can feel the dampness rising from the earth, collecting on my cheeks as dew. Last night, we slept beneath the stars, each one twinkling as bright as my hopes to find my mother. And I can't help gazing into the star-like cracks at the center of this ruby in my hand, wondering if she's somehow in there.

"Alessia," I whisper low enough not to wake Creek, "are you here? Have you left your body—are you in the stone, too?"

But the ruby feels cold, as asleep as the rest of the camp. Sighing, I stare up at the sky and the seeping blue color that's slowly becoming vibrant enough to wipe out the stars. The sky's so vast and unbroken here that it practically gives me vertigo, as if I've fallen into a glass-like sea, and I hold onto fistfuls of grass to keep my bearings. I've never slept on the ground before—at Bender Lake, Creek and I always used his platform high in a tree. All around us are young people on blankets, messy-haired children and teens who're less than twenty years old, I guess, and I wonder if that's a gypsy custom for them to sleep outside. The rest of the camp are in old fashioned wagons or small trailers tucked up against the trees, hidden from dust and wind. There are no cars here— their sturdy piebald horses with legs as large as tree trunks appear to pull everything. I can hear the horses stomping and nickering already for breakfast. But so far, I'm the only soul who's up.

Except for that strange gypsy woman.

I spy her from the corner of my eye, and it makes me jump.

Her back is to me, her raven hair delicately highlighted by the rising sun, and she's picking tender shoots in a glen in the woods and placing them in a suede pouch. Each time she plucks one, she whispers *gestena* to it as if to say "thank you."

Then she turns around to face me, as though she could feel my eyes on her back.

And smiles.

A light breeze brushes her wild hair from her face, revealing dark eyes as large as chips of coal. She pulls her coat tighter around herself, and for the first time I realize it has brass buttons that match the gold in her teeth. As the shy sun begins to warm her high cheekbones, strong nose, and full lips, I feel my breath catch.

Honest to God, she is the most beautiful woman I've ever seen.

Her features are smoothly carved—even regal—yet she seems so strong with her earthy, wide hips and straight back that funnel into a narrow waist. She reminds me of a bohemian Sophia Loren, the actress I saw in that dorky *Houseboat* movie with Cary Grant, one of the few films they let us watch at my old boarding school because it's rated G.

But something in this woman's eyes tells me she isn't rated G at all...

She narrows her eyes, her gaze intense as black beads, and lifts her chin.

"Do you want to be a girl—or a woman?" she challenges me.

I have no idea what she's talking about. But I glance back at Creek, still as a stone with scruffy bed hair on our faded blanket, and I feel unbearably naked near this woman. Something about her seems like she can see right through me. I'm still trying to wrap my head around the fact that I'm actually 18. And all of a sudden I remember—so is Creek! Today's his birthday, and we're both…adults…now.

"I already am a woman," I reply defiantly, standing up and thrusting my fists into my pockets. Second guessing myself, I realize that must look childish, so I leave the ruby in my front pocket and fold my arms. "What's it to you?"

She smiles, flashing gold teeth.

"Everything," she calls back.

Her voice rings across a nearby field and I hear birds sing in reply. She swings her pouch from her hand, back and forth like a ticking clock, as if pondering my future, then waves me over to her.

"Now come with me."

I forget to breathe.

This woman scares the daylights out of me. And I don't know if she's after the ruby in my pocket, or if she has darker intentions. How'd she know it was there? I blush, recalling it's not like I hid the bulge or anything. Swiftly, I transfer the stone to my cleavage inside my bra while she's not looking, where it feels icy against my skin. The woman is walking ahead of me deeper into the woods, taking long, swinging strides.

I feel an irresistible pull to follow her, even without Creek for protection, the same way Alice must have tumbled after that rabbit and down a hole to Wonderland. What does this woman want to show me? There's something magnetic about her—as if she stands at the gateway between my horrible and lonely teenage years and what I hope for in adulthood. And despite any logic, I feel my feet stepping after her in a way that sends violin chords screeching through my brain.

*What the hell are you doing?* Some rational part of me scolds. *This woman might want to kill you for the ruby…*

But I can't seem to get my brain to tell my feet that. My heart is racing, yet my soul is heading like a moth to a flame—her flame. And whether my brain wants to admit it or not, my soul suspects she might lead the way to Alessia.

With that thought, I feel the stone warm against my breast, pulsing to the rhythm of my strides. Cautiously, I follow this woman to a lush draw in the woods filled with green grass beside a stream.

"We flow, like this water," the woman says without turning around. "That is our nature. The life of travelers."

She stands facing the stream with her eyes closed, as if listening to it. A little girl from the camp skips up to her—with an almond complexion and bright ribbons dangling from her dreadlocks—and gives her a handful of herbs. The woman opens her eyes and smiles before the girl scampers off, swift as a breeze. Then she points to where the little girl had paused. She leans down and collects a fistful of green shoots and sniffs them before bringing them to her lips. One by one, she tastes each at the root, chewing slowly as if they were tobacco. She spits them out and nods, slipping the remaining herbs into her pouch.

"Tell me," she says softly, "what shape will the *shon*—the moon—be tonight?"

I shake my head.

"How would I know?" I answer, glancing up at the glare from the sun higher now in the sky. "It's broad daylight."

"Sit down."

I do so reluctantly, wondering how many demands this odd woman is going to make. The fact that she sits beside me makes me feel even more awkward. She crosses her legs, revealing weathered, lace-up boots, a lot like Granny Tinker's.

"Feel with your hands."

She begins swishing her fingers through the weeds.

I move my palms across the long stems that are moist with dew.

"What do you feel?"

"Um," I mutter, wondering if this is some kind of test, "wet plants, I guess. Is there more?"

The woman's broad hands pause over the grassy tips, and I thought I heard her mumble as if praying over them. Her lips rise with a hint of smile.

"The moon is full tonight. Like you."

I don't know why, but her words shoot tingles up my back.

She pets the stems lovingly, as if they're her friends. "They swell and lean toward the moon at this time, when she's round and bright. You are eighteen, no?"

The tingles are skittering in downright ripples across my skin now. I shift uncomfortably.

"H-How do you know that?" I ask, as spooked by this woman as I was when I first met Granny Tinker. Maybe more—

I feel her strong, warm hands move across my arm. Startled, I look down and see her fingers following the contours of my skin, gently kneading my flesh the way one tests a plump piece of fruit.

"I can feel your ripeness." She takes a deep breath. "Smell your—how do they say it? Your readiness."

Those gold teeth flash again with a smile. She turns her face up to the sun.

"It is time for you to show me that you can be the next *Thagarni*. Gypsy Queen."

My heart is racing out of control. And I fear at any minute it might burst through my chest like a runaway train.

"W-Wait a minute," I defend. "I don't want to be anyone's Gypsy Queen—"

The woman laughs.

"What makes you think you have a choice, *shebari?*"

"Who are you? What's your name?" I demand, standing up and glaring at her. I'm sick to death of wasting time and she's getting downright creepy. "Tell me what happened to Alessia—"

A blue bird flutters in front of my face, scaring me out of my wits.

I take a step back, hoping to make my heart rate slow down, only to see it land on the woman's arm. She and the bird are so calm in this odd moment that I half-suspect she has this animal trained. My thoughts are confirmed when I see her sneak it a bread crumb from her riding coat pocket. Strangely enough, she never looks at the bird, which I'm sure now is a kind of falcon. Nevertheless, it chortles at her and she nods, making soft sounds deep in her throat as though they share a secret language.

"If you don't lead yourself," the woman says in a peculiar tone, almost as if taking dictation from the bird, "someone else will. And you will not like the path they choose for you." She lifts her arm and lets the bird take to the air. "It's time to be a woman," she says like a warning.

We watch the bird spiral into the sky.

"Now, show me how you will make your own path."

Path to what? I wonder. The next gypsy camp, or maybe to find my mom?

"Only if you tell me your name," I insist. I'm totally done with this woman's puzzling games. Trade for a trade—I'm not my father's daughter for nothing. And if she wants me to take a fricking walk with her to find herbs or whatever and pretend I'm her long lost Gypsy Queen before telling me my mother's whereabouts, so be it. I'm as fine an actress as they come. But she'd better deliver.

The woman points to the bird over the horizon, its wings gently riding on the growing thermals of the brightening sun. It disappears into the boughs of a tall tree across a field.

"That's who I am," she replies, waving at the sky and then the earth. "My name is Zuhna. Like my friend the *falco cuculo* —I am wherever my feet land."

She stands up in front of me, but her dark eyes are still lifted to the sky, which I find peculiar. Before I can blink, she wraps a yellow paisley scarf over my eyes and ties it tight—

Holy shit!

I'm blindfolded. I whip to my feet, punching at the air, and attempt to rip off the scarf, but her strong arms are already wrapped around me like a bear. Wriggling fiercely, I can't get loose, and just when I'm about to scream Creek's name, Zuhna nearly suffocates me with her thick-skinned palm. Her seal is so strong I can't open my lips to bite her.

Seriously? I'm going to meet my death wrestling a creepy gypsy chick?

I kick back at her but she doesn't budge. Doesn't yelp. She only chuckles at me.

"Oh *dragă*, I've been kicked by wilder horses than you." She lets out a throaty laugh. "You will not get away until you follow your senses."

"My what?" I mutter, voice muffled by her fingers. At this point I'm wondering if she's got some weird fairy tale idea of preparing me for dinner.

"You want to find your mother?" she hisses, clasping me tighter.

I feel all my breath deflate from my body.

Of course that's what I want, bitch!

Tears are threatening my eyes, but I grit my teeth, ready to deck this chick the second her grip slacks.

I feel her press her suede pouch into my hand.

"Then keep this *putsi* and follow your star. Use your senses."

"Like what," I mutter, "touch, taste, smell?" My words are still garbled by her palm.

She's so close I can feel her breath against my temple. When she nestles her cheek against the back of my hair, I jump. Quite frankly, I'd love to start running by now if only I could figure out how—

"Take a deep breath," she insists, her voice low and grave.

"Then you'll tell me where my mother is?"

"No. You'll tell *yourself* where your mother is."

Her words spread a shiver through my body.

I shake my head to brush it off. For crying out loud, what's next—duck-duck-goose? It's got to be only six in the morning and this woman already has me exhausted.

"Just one sniff," Zuhna encourages.

I take a big whiff, hoping it will get her off me. At first I smell mostly her skin, a light musky scent with hints of cinnamon and clover and the earthy smell of horses. But when I inhale another deep breath, the stone trembles at my breast, and that's when I smell smoke. Grassy smoke, like a nearby meadow is on fire—

Alarmed, I reach my fingers to the scarf over my eyes, but her strong hands stop me.

"Follow," she insists, as a breeze swells up in the glen. It brings such a strong smell of smoke I start to cough.

"What kind of fool walks toward a fire?" I argue as she gently nudges me forward, her arms still wrapped around me like a vise.

"Are you so sure it's a fire?" she says.

Sighing, I take another whiff.

She's right, it smells more like…ash. As though there used to be a fire that was recently put out.

"Take a few more steps, *jel'enedra*."

I can hear her breathing deeply as well, as if catching the scent, and I wonder if she has her eyes closed, too. We step through the grass and she loosens her grip, her hands now firmly on the back of my shoulders. We go over a little hill and down into another glen. I know it's in the trees because I feel colder, as if we've stepped into a shaded, woodsy area. But when I feel the sun on my forehead again, I assume we must have reached a clearing. The stone shivers at my breast—not warm this time, but oddly freezing. It's such a shock to my skin that I rip the scarf off my face before Zuhna can stop me.

And that's when I see the blackened patches of earth. In a small meadow that's so familiar it nearly knocks the wind out of me.

This is the same place where I had my vision of the lovers who were murdered.

And I swear to God, the burned grassy area in front of me looks like two people lying on the ground holding hands, with smoke rising all around them as though they'd fallen here and were incinerated in place. The sight is beyond ghastly, like accidently stumbling into Auschwitz, and my hands rise to my mouth as I scream.

Zuhna hugs me—it's the first truly compassionate thing I've seen her do—and she rips the scarf from my hand and tosses it into the meadow, where it bursts into flames. The sight startles me and I shake all over.

"Shh," she purrs kindly, rocking me a little. "You did it, *pakvora*. You felt your way through the cracks." Just as she says that, the stone at my breast warms again.

And the blackened earth is gone—

Even the yellow paisley scarf lies on top of a few wildflowers, completely unscathed.

"Never forget," she says, "you are nothing without learning to feel. This is where your power lies—what will lead you to your mother. You must feel your way through the cracks of the star…through the folds of emotion and time."

Zuhna begins talking softly in her gypsy tongue. Not to me, but as if there's already a conversation going on with someone I can't see. With every word she utters, the stone at my breast grows warmer. I watch her nod, as though she'd retrieved a missing piece of a puzzle.

"You must be a woman to find a woman," she says to me gravely. "Not a little girl. But it comes with a price."

I don't know what the hell she means.

"How do you know my mother is *alive* in Italy somewhere and not dead?" I demand.

Zuhna tilts her head back and laughs, her smile a mix of gapped teeth and gold, with a broad cackle that eerily reminds me of Granny Tinker.

"Gypsy Queens can never truly die," she says mysteriously. She reaches out her fingers to lift my chin. "Can you handle what you find?"

My fists tighten into balls.

Who the hell is she kidding?

I've already survived a childhood in mean-girl boarding schools, an absent dad, robbing banks, and now people who've been shooting at me! I think I got this fucking covered.

"I can handle anything," I hiss back at her.

Zuhna runs her hand over my hair, stroking me like a horse.

"You are strong—so strong, young one." She cups my cheek. "It is in your soul."

Then she runs her fingers over my forehead and slowly down my temple to my cheek and jaw, her hand lingering and massaging a little, as if detecting something.

"You have tasted your lover's blood," she nods. "It's written on your face. But when he tastes yours, you will be a woman and he will be a man. And then you will come into your full power..." Her voice trails off, as if she's thinking for a moment. "You can never go back, *pisliskurja*."

She reaches into her pocket and glances back up at me. "Use your talents wisely," she warns.

With that, Zuhna holds up the ruby heart.

I choke back surprise—

I never felt her take it! Her gypsy pickpocket skills must be legendary.

I stare into her eyes for either mischief or deceit, but instead what I find are dark pools that appear like an abyss in the middle. Instinctively, I wave my hand in front of her. Nothing registers—no flutter of the lashes or eye movement.

And for the first time, I realize that Zuhna is blind.

"We all have our *segreti*—our secrets," Zuhna nods. "I only see the sun and moon, things that shine very bright. Like you." She cups my face in her hands and kisses both cheeks, in that odd way that Old World people do, and drops the stone back into my cleavage. It burns like a fire. "I also feel heat," she says, turning to walk away.

Just then, the little girl with dreadlocks scampers up to her from behind a tree, as if she'd been spying on us all along. And part of me wonders if she's for real, or if she's one of Zuhna's familiars. But then she grabs Zuhna's hand and they swing their arms in rhythm with their strides. The little girl holds up another fistful of herbs and smiles proudly.

Zuhna pauses and turns around.

"Time for breakfast," she says, tousling the little girl's hair.

"We have much work to do." She lifts her head and stares in my direction, as if she can actually see me.

"And tell your man not to follow me anymore," she calls out, pulling a silver dagger from inside her boot and flashing it to the sun.

"Or I shall have to kill him."

## 10

C reek drops from a tree right in front of me, scaring me out of my mind.

"Don't worry, babe. She wouldn't have a chance at offing me."

Cocky as hell, his lips curl crookedly, turning his cheek scar into a dagger that rivals Zuhna's, and he folds his arms. A shaft of light warms his wayward blondee hair, making his blue eyes sparkle.

"She's blind as a bat, you know, like Lorraine at Turtle Shores. But that doesn't mean she doesn't see things—"

"Creek!" I gasp. "You were watching this whole time?"

"Of course. You don't think I'd let you out of my sight, do you?"

I swallow him in a kiss.

A hot, impulsive, grab-your-face kiss. The kind that says *Thank God you're here, because I don't think I could last another minute without you.*

"Mmm…" he sighs, stroking my back and relishing my rare vulnerability. Beneath my lips, I can feel his stretch into a smile. "Miss me?"

Goose bumps dance across my skin. Not just because I'm liplocked with the handsomest guy I've ever known, and he smells as fresh as the open air and grass we slept on last night, but because Zuhna's right—I'm as ripe as they come. I can feel my desire for him moistening parts of my body I hardly knew existed, filling the cool morning air with heat. But also with relief that I'm not alone with Zuhna anymore.

Creek presses his chest against mine, as if to prove my point. My nipples stretch to meet him, greeting the hardness of his body. But then he wraps his arms around me, sensing how frightened I really was to be away from him in the camp.

"She couldn't hurt you, Robin," he whispers into my hair. "Not with me around. That's why I let you go off with her. I wanted to hear what she'd say."

"You saw me walk away with her and everything?

"I always keep track of you, remember? That's how we met—I was your stalker." His lips reach into a smile. "It was fun."

I sock his arm. That arm, the one with *Partners* carved into it.

"Ow!" He yelps, laughing and rubbing his bicep.

"You let me think I was all alone with that crazy gypsy chick?"

"I wanted to see what she would show you."

All of a sudden, I remember that I still have Zuhna's suede pouch in my hand—the one she claimed helped guide me to the scorched meadow. Or I should say, formerly scorched meadow that's now perfectly green. "Did you, um...see anything?" I ask Creek.

He falls silent. But I notice his cool blue eyes flicker a little.

"I don't see what you and Zuhna see," he admits, thrusting his hands in his pockets.

The irony's not lost on me, considering Zuhna's blindness.

"But that doesn't mean I can't tell what's happening to you."

In that moment, I feel as transparent as glass, as though Creek sees through me more clearly than Zuhna. He glances down at the pouch in my hand and then looks at me strangely, as if something about me has changed.

And God as my witness, I can taste his blood in my mouth again, that blend of iron and copper and soul. I try and swallow to force it away, but it doesn't work.

Is that the difference? I wonder. Are we linked now more than ever before—because I took a lick of my true love's blood?

"Creek," I sputter, "do you think I really am the next..."

I can't get the words "Gypsy Queen" out of my mouth. It's too damn weird.

Creek presses his palms over my temples, staring into my eyes.

And I realize something about him has changed, too.

He's a man, now—eighteen—all grown up.

And the daylight has become stark, revealing every scar and burn mark on his skin from his horrendous childhood, along with the tattoo of a snake winding down his forearm that he got to cover it all up. What used to look devil-may-care about him to me now seems as hard as a soldier who was simply hiding beneath his happy-go-lucky front. We're alike, he and I. We had to grow up fast in our own ways. But what does the future hold for us now?

"Robin," he whispers, tracing his finger slowly around my head like an invisible tiara. He runs his hand gently down my neck to the stone heart that's buried between my breasts, where he lets his fingers linger. "You were always a queen in my book."

I blush, feeling the heat suffuse from the stone through my breasts and into my entire being. Arching my back toward him, I wish I could have him here—right now—for breakfast. But for this moment, I let his warm hand pulse inside my bra, seeking one breast and then the other, tenderly pressing my nipples. White sparks overtake my vision as the sensation makes me soar…

I swipe another kiss. "Happy birthday, baby," I breathe, feeling the blood swell in my chest.

A shrill cry cuts through the air like a wild bird, giving me a start. I hear the sound of violins rise, low and mournful at first, then swirling in elegant notes to a brighter tune.

Creek smiles. He leans in and draws a slow breath, as if to inhale my essence for a second, and gently removes his fingers from my skin. He kisses my breastbone with soft lips before readjusting my shirt so no one can spy the stone heart.

"C'mon," he sighs, "I think they have plans for us."

"Plans?" I reply as he grabs my hand. "What plans?"

Creek smirks. "You'll see. We're not as far from Turtle Shores as you might think."

We walk toward the camp, where it's obvious that everyone is up now, folding blankets, feeding horses, and chasing chickens and children. But what I didn't expect are the whimsical decorations that run from wagon to wagon that seem to match the light and airy violins. Thin wires coil around little ceramic pots holding lit candles, which hang between the wagons and trees, sparkling around the camp like stars. The sight is so lovely it makes me gasp.

"Do they always celebrate daybreak like this?" I ask Creek, just now noticing the colorful scarves that dangle from tree branches, waving in the breeze like wings.

Creek shrugs. "No. I think they consider this a kind of holiday."

When he gives me a wink, it takes a second for it to sink in.

"Because it's your birthday?" I ask, floored. "How would they know?"

Creek stares at Zuhna's pouch in my hand again, lifting his gaze to the tree limbs to spy the last thin outline of the round moon in the sky. He reaches down and rips up a handful of weeds with a pretty wildflower in the center and holds it out to me.

"Weren't you listening to Zuhna?" He replies. "The gypsies know, the same way they know everything—by feeling the days and seasons. The ripeness of things."

He tastes one of the shoots at the root the way Zuhna did. "Hmm, not bad," he smirks. "Might make a half decent tea. With leaves that can tell the future, like birthdays."

Could he sound more like Granny Tinker? I marvel, wondering if spooky redneck sorcery runs in his family, too. He lets the grasses fall through his fingers, but tucks the delicate wildflower tenderly behind my ear. Then he plays with a curl of my hair for a moment before taking a step back.

My heart nearly stops at the way his eyes admire what he sees.

You would've thought I was in that silver gown again with him at a ball in Cincinnati, the way his eyes shine, tracing along each curve of my face and body. And I can't help stealing a glance at my sneakers, half-expecting them to turn into glass, and wondering if the nearby horses were once field mice. Meeting each other's gaze, we both feel it. This potent moment in a slightly secluded glen near the camp, both of us on the cusp of blossoming into something grown up— something altogether new.

And there's my Creek. Tall, handsome, gallant as always, with that big crooked grin on his face, looking at me as if I'm his star.

The music echoes lightly around us, and he holds out his hand.

"Dance?" he whispers. The yearning in his eyes steals my heart for eternity.

You goddamn thief, I think to myself, smiling inside. Each day you swipe everything I've got in my soul all over again.

I hesitate, wanting to remember him this way—so beautiful and perfect and into me, with no one else in the world watching, except for maybe that little girl who's always spying behind trees. This is *us* before we face the rest of our lives. I inhale a deep breath and lift my chin.

"Always," I smile, taking his hand.

He holds me close, swaying his hips in time with mine in

the glen. The song the violins are playing is foreign to me and a touch exotic, with sharp and sometimes lonely notes, but so rich it practically fills me to my bones. And I feel a shudder from the stone at my breast.

All at once, I realize this is what Martiya didn't get to do—dance with her one true love in the glen before she was murdered, before their bodies were set on fire. Their lives—their love—were cut short.

"That's not going to be me," I whisper darkly like I'm cursing at the stone. I push it deeper into my cleavage with my fingers to stop its wobble. "Creek and I are going to make it."

"What?" Creek says. He keeps his hips swaying in motion, but tips up my chin, puzzled.

"You and me—we're forever, right? Come what may?"

Creek envelops me in a kiss, wrapping his arms around my body.

He speaks no words, letting his closeness and the music do all the talking. When the violins stop for a second, he leans his forehead against mine.

"Forever for me began the very moment I set eyes on you. I *protect* what I love, Robin."

And to my surprise, he snatches Zuhna's pouch from my hand and opens it, brazenly scattering all of her herbs and wildflowers around us in a circle. Tossing the pouch into the tall grass, he encases me in his arms again, holding tight, as if he's never letting go.

His nose barely touches mine, but those blue eyes of fractured ice look as if they're melting right through me.

"Robin, I already have everything I've ever wanted," he

whispers, low and intense, as if draining his soul into mine. "And there ain't no gypsy spell on earth that's gonna get past me. As far as I'm concerned, eighteen is looking pretty damn fantastic."

I close my eyes, letting his words ring in my ears, ring in my soul. But then I hear a swift shuffling through the grass, followed by odd mumbles.

When my eyes flutter open, I spot a red-haired woman coming at us with a broom. She's muttering in a tongue that's doesn't sound gypsy or like anything else I recognize. She starts brushing at us, scooting us faster with her broom toward the camp.

"*Dolgozik!*" She cries. "Time to eat! Work!"

We laugh at each other a little, then sigh and follow after her toward the fireplace between the wagons, which holds the black pot with steam rising. A row of children are huddled around it, munching on what appear to be hot cakes. They smell divine. I'm so hungry now that's all my mind can focus on, and the red-haired woman drops her broom and fishes out a couple of cakes with a stick from the black pot for Creek and I. Wolfing down the first bite, it nearly scalds my tongue—but the taste is out of this world. Within a few more bites, my mouth is an explosion of almond and vanilla, and the light sweetness goes to my head.

I reach in my hand for another, tossing the cake between my palms as it cools. I hear laughter as I greedily stuff it into my mouth.

"Good, ya?" says a blonde, portly woman across the fire. She has bright cheeks and braids over her head and looks

Swedish or German—and that's when I truly notice some of the other gypsies. Since we arrived at nightfall yesterday, I assumed everyone was dark haired and tan. But now, in broad daylight, I realize this isn't a traditional gypsy band at all. A few men and woman look Romanian or Hungarian, like you'd expect, but the rest are blonde, red-haired, fair or freckled—as though they've come together from all over Europe. The one thing they have in common are their creative clothes. There's lots of ribbon and embroidery and crazy-quilt-style patches, as if bright colors are highly valued. And though they sometimes seem to be muttering in different languages, a welcoming smile is universal.

Creek nudges next to me, chomping on another hot cake. "You remember the trailer park at Turtle Shores, right? How the misfits all banded together to make a family." He nods his head at a man walking by with an awkward limp. "Here, they've found their family, too."

"So I'm the heir apparent to the…misfits?" I smirk, remembering all the charming crazies at Turtle Shores—the only people I've ever known in my life who made me feel like I belonged.

Creek slings his arm around me. "Not much has changed, sweetheart," he laughs. But his eyes soften at the sight of a few old men seated beside a wagon who softly stroke their violins with bows, filling the air with a profound beauty. Some of them don't have teeth or hair, and one has a patch over his eye. But together, they make the morning sound exquisite.

"*Poshrats*," I hear a soft, familiar voice say. Turning around, I see Zuhna again. She's holding a leather apron in one hand,

and her empty suede pouch in the other, with a smile curling over gold teeth. The sight of it makes me blush, and I hope we didn't offend her. "We are the wanderers," she says. "Some are *zingari*—gypsy. Others only part, or not at all. But we all travel. And work."

She turns and points to a silver Airstream trailer beneath a tree, surprisingly modern in this setting. But next to it is a burly man with an anvil on a tree stump, pounding out horseshoes.

"You—time to get busy," she nods at Creek, handing him the leather apron. "Your woman comes with me."

My eyes grow wide, wondering what she has in mind. I watch Creek walk off to the blacksmith, tying the apron around his neck and back before he sneaks a look over his shoulder to check if I'm all right. With a deep breath, I give him a nod and follow after Zuhna to an old-fashioned wagon, painted red on top with lovely scroll designs on the sides beside its door. All around us are other traveling people on chairs and tree stumps, stitching blankets, stringing beads for jewelry, sharpening knives, or tooling leather. These are the wares they'll eventually sell at markets, I assume. When we reach the wooden steps of the wagon, Zuhna pats her hand to feel for the wrought-iron handle and opens the door wide.

"Come, it's time for you to stop looking like an American," she says gravely, inviting me inside. "I'm sure they're already trying to find you."

A chill works its way down my spine.

"They?" I reply to test her.

"Alessia's family," she says impatiently, walking up the steps. "They always try to destroy the Gypsy Queen."

"What did they do with her?" I scamper into the wagon

filled with an old stove and quilts and pillows, a lot like Granny Tinker's. "Did they dump her in an institution in the mountains? Where is it—"

Zuhna merely pats the stone at my breast. I flush with embarrassment, realizing she knows it's still there.

"You will see after tonight. And then you will go find her."

"How?" I ask breathlessly, but she places her finger gently on my lips.

"In time. You must get ready now."

For the love of God, sometimes I want to slap her. But she's blind, and I can't exactly draw a map to Alessia's whereabouts myself. I have to wait and trust her instincts. I can hear the ringing of Creek's hammer against the anvil outside, and I still wish he was with me as a buffer against Zuhna's spookiness. Just as I'm about to open my mouth and suggest I go out there to help him, Zuhna cuts me off.

"Strip," she says. "Your clothes. Now."

She heads to the wagon door and shuts it.

Before I can utter a word, she's turns and lifts my t-shirt over my head.

"W-What—why?" I stutter, shocked by her boldness. Her fingers are working nimbly at my jeans button, in spite of my efforts to push away her hands.

"You hush, and behave your-self," she orders, tossing aside my sneakers. She feels her way to a bench cabinet and opens it up, pulling out a skirt and pretty cotton blouse with bell sleeves.

It's a lovely peasant blouse, embroidered with intricate chains of flowers and leaves over the yoke. I notice that

Zuhna's face softens, becoming more tender than I've ever seen before, and it just about breaks my heart.

Was this hers as a younger woman, or maybe her daughter's once? Something about its soft and pristine cotton seems like an heirloom.

Whatever the case, I can tell Zuhna's attached to it, and it's no small gesture that she's giving it to me. For a traveling woman of few possessions, this blouse might very well be one of the most treasured things she owns.

She cradles the fabric in her arms and holds it out to me like an offering.

"Here, this was mine once. On my wedding day."

I pause, my mouth falling slack, hesitant to accept it.

"Zuhna," I protest, "I can't take something so valuable from you. Don't you have another gypsy-style blouse or anything?"

"Do you love him?"

The blush that travels from my cheeks to the rest of my body with lightning speed surprises me in its prickling heat.

I remain quiet for a moment.

"Of course I do," I reply breathlessly, as if it's something I'm ready to fight for. "With everything I've got—"

"Good," she nods. "Then you wear this tonight."

There's no arguing with Zuhna. With her shoulders held back and her mouth in a straight line, she hands the blouse to me whether I like it or not. I smile a little, running my fingers over the intricate embroidery that feels like silk.

"Thank you," I whisper, still not quite comprehending her generosity. Out of respect for her, I climb out of my jeans and into the skirt she's pulled out, then look around. There's a pair of leather boots on the floor—with rounded toes and a buckle on the side like motorcyclists wear. They'll have to do.

"Do I look gypsy enough yet?" I ask her, suddenly realizing my mistake. My cheeks burn hot.

Zuhna just laughs—a long, deep cackle, filling the wagon.

"Ya," she nods. She smoothes my skirt down over my hips and pats down the puffiness of my sleeves. Then she sets her hands on my shoulders. "But you need one more thing."

As she unbuttons her riding coat, I get a better look at her clothes, too. Her blouse is maroon with ruffles beneath a black vest appliqued with birds, moons, and stars. Her wide hips fit into a tiered, midnight blue skirt. Casting off her coat, she works a stack of silver and gold bangles from her wrist, and before I can stop her, her strong hands grab my arm and slip the bangles onto mine.

I gasp at her extraordinary generosity.

"But Zuhna—"

"Sit down, my dear gypsy," she interrupts me. I'm not quite certain, but I thought I saw tears well in her dark eyes. She gently pats my head.

I lower myself onto the wood bench covered with pillows built into the side of the wagon, listening to the sweet tone of the bangles jingling. They slowly warm against my wrist

"Now," she says, sitting across from me behind the small table in the center. "We look at your next life."

"Life?" I say, expecting her to bring out a deck of tarot cards to tell my fortune like Granny Tinker did.

"You will go from being a child to a woman tonight. Someone who charts her own course. But will you lead the stone, or will it lead you?" She grabs a brass candlestick and feels for a box of matches, opening it and striking one to give the candle a light.

"I thought you said I need the stone to find my mother," I reply, feeling its weight acutely against my chest.

"Truth. But it also needs you," she says mysteriously. Which one will rule?"

I have no idea what she's driving at, but my heart skips a beat as she boldly grabs the stone from my cleavage.

"Look at the heart," she says, holding it out on her palm. "What do you see?"

The flame from the candle makes the ruby glisten. "Just cracks in the middle," I reply, wondering if this is some kind of Rorschach test. "They make a kind of star."

"You will see much more soon, *shebari*. This is the star that will lead you home," she smiles. "If you're brave enough to go. Now we make you look like woman."

With that, she blows out the candle. In the dim wagon light, I can see her smudging her finger against the blackened wick.

"Lean your head back," she says, "and close your eyes."

When I do, she traces her finger gently along the lashes of my eyelids, then underneath my eyes as well.

"You rest now, because tonight you will need all your energy." She fluffs up some pillows and sets them on the bench. Then she pulls out an old blanket and lays it over my lap.

"Here, fix the holes in this blanket while you wait." She points to a small fabric cushion on the table pricked with needles attached to thread. "When it's time, we come get you." she says. Zuhna walks to the end of the wagon and opens the door, flooding it with daylight. When she closes it again, I hear the click of the lock.

Its finality makes me jump.

And after that, there's empty silence—except for Zuhna's footsteps that fade as she walks away. And the sound of her low voice, singing.

## 11

I've been in the wagon all afternoon, stitching up rips and broken seams on the blanket and feeling like that poor girl in *Rumpelstiltskin* who was forced to spin for hours, except I haven't spotted any gold yet. From the small windows, I can tell the sun is starting to go down. It's a good thing I ate so many hot cakes, because I haven't touched food since breakfast. For the first time all day, the blacksmith's hammer has stopped clanging, and the violins have begun to fill the air again. But there's something more—a low chorus of gentle voices coming from the camp, with deep, undulating tones, as if their earthy song helps bring on the darkening sky. The candles they've strung together twinkle in the growing shadows, as though encouraging the stars to come out. When the door handle finally turns to my wagon, I leap to my feet.

That little girl with ribbons and dreadlocks in her hair peeks in her head.

"*Cheros!* Time!" she says excitedly, waving her hands.

I follow her outside, where I can see most of the gypsies gathered around the fire. In the distance, Creek is still helping to shoe one of the piebald horses. He's wearing a tweed cap now and a white, v-neck gypsy shirt along with black trousers and boots. His sleeves are all rolled up, revealing every taut muscle, and he's hammering shoes onto an unruly stallion that matches him with its wild, sinewy beauty. As the breeze picks up and rifles through the horse's black and white mane, it rears up, snorting red nostrils and striking hooves in air. Rather than dash for cover, like the other gypsy man, Creek merely drops the iron shoe and seizes the horse's halter, speaking softly to him. The stallion paws the ground with his head bowed, as if listening, but then rears a couple more times to show off his massive strength. Creek simply smiles, giving the stallion just enough lead to release his pent up energy and flex his muscles before Creek gently strokes his neck and rubs between his ears. The stallion tosses his head one last time, but then burrows his muzzle into Creek's chest.

I smile to myself. It's no surprise to me this willful beast feels comfortable around Creek. He has a knack for letting wild things stay wild, and embracing them just the way they are.

The breeze rises again. Creek straightens his back and lifts his head, turning a little as if listening to it. And I swear to God, it's as though he feels me before he sees me. He swivels around and stares straight across the camp, laying eyes on me as though he knew I'd be there.

And I wish I could frame that look on his face.

The setting sun reflects across his hat and cheekbones and the horse's neck and mane, as if they'd both been dipped in gold. The way he stares at me is not the look of a teenager anymore. It's the gaze of a young man—recognizing the love of his life.

The burly blacksmith grabs the horse's lead and gestures for Creek to walk over to me. But this is no mere stroll. More like a male rite of passage, because as soon as he nears the campfire the men of the camp grab him and shove a bottle of wine in his hand, threading their arms over each other's shoulders for a boisterous line dance. They laugh and pass the bottle around along with a pipe as the violin melody hastens to keep up with their feet. The little girl shows me a sweet ring of flowers she'd picked and tugs on my hand for me to bend down. She places the garland over my head and shrieks with glee.

"Come!" The blonde portly woman cries, running up and taking me by the arm. "We dance!"

All this for Creek's birthday? I marvel, suspecting ulterior motives by now. I glance down at my pretty pleasant blouse— the one Zuhna wore for her own wedding—and feel my cheeks blush.

The women are in a line opposite of the men on the other side of the campfire with their arms interlocked, kicking up their heels. Children are clapping and spinning in place, some waving bright scarves. Then a little boy holds up a hollowed loaf of bread and gives a loud cry. While dancing, the men pull coins from their pockets and toss them, spinning expertly, into the bread and congratulate each other on their aim. The boy lays the bread loaf right in front of me beside the campfire. Then the little girl with dreadlocks breaks over to the men's side of the dance and shoves Creek toward me, making everyone laugh. To my surprise, she pulls a long red ribbon out of her pocket and begins winding it around us, singing chants.

I'm so overwhelmed by this display that I'm sure my face is as red as her ribbon. Sensing my self-consciousness, Creek sweetly cups his palms around my cheeks, but it only makes the camp hoot louder.

"Looks like we've stumbled into something more than a birthday party." He smiles, gazing into my eyes. "I think this is their version of…you know…a gypsy wedding—"

What I see reflected in Creek's face is not the cocky expression I've grown accustomed to. Though his eyes twinkled just moments ago, right now they're dead serious. And their blue ice appears to be searching mine, as if trying to find some sign of…forever?

How could I not melt?

Even the stone at my breast is throbbing to the staggered beats of my heart.

I glance around the camp, but the dancing has ceased for a moment. Everyone is looking at us, waiting and holding their breath.

I pull the ruby heart from my blouse and hold it up to Creek, the flames of the fire dancing at its center, conscious of the ribbon that binds us together.

"Creek—right here, right now—I couldn't walk away from you if my life depended on it. You *are* my heart."

"Does that mean we're more than partners?" he asks.

I swear I saw his Adam's apple wobble. He puts his hands around mine, but they're not timid or nervous, like I expected. They're warm and strong—and determined.

"When I give my heart, Robin, it's for keeps," Creek

promises. "And I'm a hell of a lot more relentless than any damn stone."

Tears are moistening my eyes. And I'm not quite sure, but I thought I saw sparks fly in the middle of the ruby heart.

"I want you," I say like a vow to Creek. "My love is for all time."

I lean in and steal a kiss.

I thought the camp would howl in triumph, but instead they all look toward Zuhna. She gives them a nod and steps up to me. From her pocket she pulls out a long silver chain.

"You know what you choose, yes?" She says not to me, but to Creek.

Her veiled-looking brown eyes bore into him, even though I know she can't see. And to my astonishment, she snatches the ruby heart from my hand and strings the silver chain through the small clasp at the top of the stone. Then she laces it not around my neck, but around Creek's, and fastens it like a necklace—or a heavy weight, depending on how you look at it.

"Do you accept this burden?" she asks Creek, her tone ominous. The camp is so quiet now you could hear a pin drop.

Creek lifts his head and smiles.

He doesn't glance at the stone. He stares straight into my eyes with every ounce of conviction he has in him.

"It's what keeps me *alive*," he replies, his voice a mix of both hope and gravel.

Zuhna nods and throws up her hands. A raw cry erupts from her chest, resounding among the trees. "*Abiav!*" she announces, picking up her skirt and launching into a jig with an abandon that amazes me, given her eyesight. It's as if her feet already know what to do, where to go, and the other women laugh and pat me on the back and follow suit. Then the men light up more pipes and begin to dance again as well, while other members of the camp go to fetch food—piles of it! They bring out a table loaded with breads, potatoes, chicken and sauces that smell of wild mushrooms and herbs. My mouth is watering, but a boy hands me a bottle of wine before I can even think of heading to the feast.

I cautiously take a sip.

It's sweet and bubbly, and immediately goes to my head.

"Prosecco," the boy says proudly before he darts off to join in the dance.

I glance at the bottle in my hand and its words in Italian, not knowing if it was purchased from a nearby vineyard, or stolen? How fitting for a couple of lovestruck thieves.

"A toast?" I say to Creek, holding up the bottle and watching the flames of the fire dance in his eyes now. A devilish look has returned to his face.

"No," he replies, shaking his head. He starts to slowly unravel the red ribbon that holds us together and swirls it gently around my neck, pulling me in for another deep kiss.

"Tonight," he whispers, "all I want is *you*."


And for the life of me, I thought I heard the ruby heart begin to laugh.

W hen it comes to touching Creek's body and my fear of the consequences of the stone, Creek's body wins.

Every time.

It's past midnight and we're in the same wagon Zuhna led me to earlier. The blanket I repaired turned out to be our wedding *pătură*, as Zuhna called it, and the wagon is a *vardo* where only adults sleep—in every sense of the word.

My head is still swimming from the music, dancing, and Prosecco. And I can't decide whether the sweetness that lingers in my mouth is the sparkling wine, or from the anticipation of tasting Creek.

Creek...

Who stands before me, his frame lit only by the wavering candles in our wagon, nearly unrecognizable in his gypsy clothes and tweed cap. But those icy wolf eyes are trained on me, hungry as hell.

I move in for the kill first—

Boldly, I trace my finger along his exposed chest at the opening of his v-neck gypsy shirt, where the ruby heart lies, red and shimmering. His tan skin trembles at my touch, and Creek closes his eyes, dipping his head a little. But every muscle in his body is tight, as if he's holding himself back from pouncing on me like prey. I can see his fists clench, broad knuckles flashing white, as though he's afraid of what the force of his desire might do to me.

And like a cat, all I want to do is play with that longing.

I'm sure he's had other girls.

But he's never touched a soul as wild as mine.

I don't know what's gotten into me—maybe it's because I tasted Creek's blood. Or maybe it's because of that goddamn stone. But right now, even though I'm a virgin who spent her life locked away in private boarding schools, I have an overwhelming urge to lick every inch of his body until he's quivering—screaming—out of control.

My tongue rolls down his chest to his nipple as the stone brushes against my temple. Creek groans softly, and that's when I hear a low whisper.

*Taste your destiny, Rubina.*

I swallow hard, my own blood pulsing at my breasts and between my legs, as if they're on fire.

*Eat him alive.*

The stone's urgings don't belong here—don't belong with me—and I shake my head to dismiss the whispers. Pressing my lips softly against Creek's skin, I relish his warmth with a hint of salt and that lingering meadow scent from sleeping outside. Slowly, I run my palms over his hard muscles, and Creek caves, bringing his hands to my waist to pull up my peasant blouse. He lifts it over my head and unclasps my bra in seconds, but then he slowly slides the straps over my shoulders until the bra falls lazily to the floor.

My breasts are exposed now, nipples outstretched, wanting him—yearning for him.

Creek leans down and simply breathes.

His soft air caresses my nipples, and he blows on them, the warmth floating across my skin like a beautiful song. I arch my back, wanting him to kiss me, devour me, but Creek only smiles.

Who's in control now?

I couldn't hear the stone's insistent murmurs if I wanted to, because the blood is hammering so hard in my brain it's driving me out of control—

"Please touch me," I whisper, aching inside.

"As you wish," Creek replies, his lips curling further. His eyes glance up at me full of power, and he fucking knows he's got me already. Blowing ever so softly, one nipple and then the other, his hands refusing to touch me yet, he slips out his tongue and gives my left breast just one, very wet lick.

And I feel every neuron in my brain pop and explode.

The other breast receives his lick, ever so gratefully.

Each breast is swept by his tongue, soft and slow, until he's fallen to his knees and pulls me to his mouth. He sucks on my breasts with a ravenous hunger, and I throw off his tweed cap and claw my hands through his hair.

His *short* hair?

Stunned, I open my eyes, not realizing they were closed

before because I was too busy drowning in the sensation of Creek's tongue.

"You cut your hair?" I gasp.

He rises to his feet, throwing off his shirt and blinding me with that beautiful, toned chest—that's filled with horrendous scars. Each one a vicious memory that he seems to be making up for now.

"I had to, baby," he replies, running his hand through his choppy hair.

I don't know how he does it, but Creek can go from molten hot to frozen cold eyes in a heartbeat, scaring the shit out of virtually anybody.

My bare nipples feel his ice, but it only makes them harden for him more.

"The de Bargonas are surely searching for us, Robin," he says. "I had to change my looks, like you did, to blend in." He smoothes the unevenness of his hair a little. "All I had was the blacksmith's old knife. What do you think?"

Seriously? He's heaven on earth as far as I'm concerned, even if he died his hair purple. But I don't let on for a moment how wildly I'm attracted to him.

"Well I don't know," I sigh, "I think I'm going to miss that beautiful hair."

"Yeah?" Creek smiles, circling my nipple with his finger.

"You know, how soft it felt in my hands."

"Like this?" Creek whispers, circling my other nipple.

His tongue starts to wrap around my breast again, while his hand runs down my curly dark hair. He stops for a second and leans his cheek into its softness before he returns to his luxurious licking, faster now, full of promise—

"I think I might be able to make you forget my hair, baby," he whispers. "Besides, it'll grow back…"

Creek said something more but I have no idea what it was. My heart is pounding hard and my body is swimming in such raw pulses that I couldn't remember the alphabet if I wanted to right now. Savagely, I dive for his trouser button and pull down his pants along with his underwear. His penis is hard, trembling, angling for me already. Creek responds in kind by sliding his warm hands down my waist and slipping the skirt—and my underwear with it—from my hips. We both kick off our boots and push our clothes aside with our feet.

For the first time ever, we're completely naked in front of each other. And Creek is so tall and muscular and beautiful that I forget to breathe.

I know I should feel self-conscious, with this god-like creature before me, but every second feels so *right* it's as though the angels created us to stand—young and beautiful and yearning—for this very moment. All Creek is wearing is that ruby stone, glistening like the powerful desire I feel between my legs. I grasp the stone at his chest and feel his penis press against my thigh.

"Are you ready for this?" I whisper. "For everything sex with me, you know, might bring?"

Boldly, I can't stop myself from fondling him—wanting to taste him already—but he moans and stops my hand.

"Not too fast, baby," Creek says. "I want you all night—all life—long."

"Even if it kills us both?" I reply. I dip down to my knees and take an unauthorized lick of his penis. Rather than stop me this time, Creek buries his hands in my hair as though it were luxurious mink.

He groans, the kind that comes soft and deep from within his chest.

God, how I love this power! I see the stone blaze bright red as I sweep my tongue over his tip, teasingly, then swallow him whole, feeling his blood pulse at my lips as if I'd somehow gripped his soul. In and out I move, relishing him like candy, until he grabs my arms and pulls me to my feet with such raw power it leaves me rattled.

No permission—taking me by force—Creek lifts me in his strong arms and carries me to the bed at the back of the wagon. He lays me down gently over the old quilts, soft as baby blankets, where his eyes travel over every inch of my body with more than desire…

With *love*.

A guy can't fake the look that's in his eyes right now.

Those glacial blue eyes are melted pools of tenderness, and it blows me away even more than his touch.

"Creek," I gasp, in love with every inch of him, but feeling oddly shy right now at the same time, like I might be pressing too hard into his secrets. "You've never—I mean, you know —told me…"

He tips his head slightly to one side. "What? That I *love* you? Baby, you've got me heart and soul—"

I swallow hard.

"No, you've never told me your last name. I mean, the *real* one."

Creek lays down as gently beside me as a panther moving in shadows, his body slinking next to mine, warm and hard.

The stone heart around his neck falls between us, hot as a hunk of coal. And for a moment I thought I saw it flash sparks.

"It's the same name as yours now, right?" he whispers, running his finger oh-so-softly down my breastbone to my navel, where he pauses before going further toward my sex. To my surprise, he opens my legs and leans his face there and breathes the word "Flynn" into the folds of my skin. Just one lick sets my nerve endings on fire, before he runs his tongue up my to my belly button all the way to my lips. He perches over me with his arms on either side, and I can see his eyes are all wondering and yearning at the same time. "Will you take my name, Robin?"

I grab his head and pull him down to me, wrapping my legs around his beautiful ass.

"Yes!" I smile before he devours me in a kiss.

The stone is hot, pressing between my breasts, but what feels far more profound is his penis, hard and pulsing, against my thigh. "I want you, Creek," I say breathlessly, squeezing him between my legs with all I've got. "Now—"

"Not yet, Mrs. Flynn," he whispers, stopping my hand as I try to touch him again. He clutches my hand in his, hard, and draws down to my sex again. "I want you to know what it feels like to be my...*wife*."

He breathed that word like the finest poetry before he slid his tongue between my thighs, dabbing up and down the folds at first until settling and undulating softly, to the beat of my own heart. Pulsing and wet, Creek drives his tongue up and down the inner lining of my skin, and I grab his cropped hair in fierce desire. This is crazy—the white hot explosions are overtaking my vision, trickling into every inch of my body like bolts of electricity. I widen my legs and pull his head down to me, groaning in pleasure so great it overtakes me almost like pain. His tongue in turns sweetly dabs at the inner folds and then rolls back and forth over my sex like a freight train. For a moment it's so powerful I lose my breath, but then I want to scream and nothing comes out. I'm becoming wasted by him. As if to show off more power, Creek inserts his tongue into my vagina and expertly brings it back out to circle the nub of my clitoris in one smooth and artful motion, again and again, until all I can see is blistering white sparks. The pleasure rolls over me, seizing every nerve and muscle, and I can't help letting out a cry.

"More!" I demand breathlessly, completely stricken by him as he reaches up his hands and fondles my nipples while his tongue is still buried in my sex, throbbing, licking, taking me for everything I'm worth. I spread my legs as wide as they can go, wanting my body to swallow him whole. And that's when I beg—

"Creek, come inside me now!" I insist. In spite of the overwhelming pleasure, I move beneath him and seize his penis in my hands. "I want you inside," I moan desperately.

But Creek's tongues seeks my nipple as his hand keeps the pleasure going between my legs, slipping his fingers up and down and driving me crazy. His finger circles me as he sucks on my breast, bringing a whole new wave of pleasure to my being. "No baby," he gasps, taking a breath. "I want you to come—full blown—before I enter you because it's your first time. I don't want anything to get in the way."

I cup my hands around his cheeks and pull his face to

mine, kissing him, even as his hand never stops working on the heaven between my thighs.

"How do you know I'm a virgin?" I whisper, arching my back, up and down, with the pleasure. My eyes are half closed with the insanity of his touch, trembling as he sinks his fingers into my vagina and then circles my clitoris again.

"Because," he says, staring at me as if I'm the only girl who ever existed, "it's written on your soul. You still have hope." He crushes his lips to mine in a take-all kind of kiss. "And that makes you beautiful. You don't have a trace of weariness for men in your eyes, Robin. And I'm for damned sure gonna keep it that way."

With that, Creek kisses my forehead, my cheek, my lips, moving between my breasts, then one for each nipple for good measure. His hand keeps working at my sex, sending shivers across my whole body as he traces kisses down my waist and to my thighs. I feel his kisses, hot and rapid, head to my sex and lick at me fiercely now. No, more than that—his lips start to swallow me whole until the waves are so intense that I'm screaming, panting, and screaming for more. All at once, I feel taken by a mighty wave so beautiful and powerful, it's as though I've been washed out to sea with sun glinting on crashes of water. The sensation leaves me shaking and gasping, and before I know it, I feel a cool circle working its way up my finger.

I can hardly see right now, but in the haze of my mad orgasm, I realize Creek has slipped a gold ring onto my finger.

"How do you like being Mrs. Flynn?" he smiles crookedly, just enough to flash that dagger scar before pressing a warm kiss to my forehead.

Stunned, I feel completely bathed in Creek's love, as if he'd spread a warm light all over my body, making every inch of my skin revel in bliss. Lifting my hand, I glance at the gold that's wrapped around my finger. "C-Creek," I stutter, where did you get this?"

He's beaming at me, eyes sparkling in mischief, and he lifts my chin with his finger and swipes another kiss.

"Thieves never reveal their secrets," Creek whispers in reply, but it's then that I realize the ring looks conspicuously like the gold earring left in the woods by our gondola guide. Except there's a pretty scroll design etched across it now with the word "Partners" stamped in the center. He winks at me, and I get an inkling that he must've conspired with the gypsy jewelry-makers while I was in the wagon today.

"Hold on for a second," Creek says as he bounds from our bed. I can hear the coins from the gypsy men's bread toss rattling in his trouser pockets as he lifts his pants to retrieve something. He's back beside me again in a moment, where I see him unwrapping a condom with Italian words printed on it.

"More stolen goods?" I giggle, marveling at his preparedness. But Creek's face grows stern.

"Robin," he whispers, putting on the condom and then tracing the hair gently from my forehead while searching my eyes. "I never want you to go through what my mom and your mom did—having babies before they really knew who they were. It turns women into ghosts. I want you, Robin, full and alive and fiery as hell."

With a wicked smirk, I grab at him and thrust him into me before he can utter another word. Wrapping my legs around

Creek, I pull him into me stronger, and he gasps as his flesh cuts through the tightness of my skin. Hitching my breath, I realize I've lost my virginity to my...

Husband.

"Oh Robin," he cries out as his muscles shift into overdrive, crazy with desire. As he pumps into me, slowly at first, our bodies combining with sweat, muscle, and heat, I feel my own inner flesh ripping apart. Its stings more than hurts, like a raw sunburn, and we sway and rock, when Creek's hand reaches down to my sex again, lovingly rubbing against me until I'm once again on fire. Another wave comes—one that totally shocks me, that I didn't know I was capable of—and completely makes me forget the sting at my vagina. I cry out, my legs encasing him tighter, swallowing him whole and abandoning myself to all that is Creek.

And that's when my vision explodes into a horizon of red.

At first I think it must be another orgasm. Yet out of the billows of crimson, I see a figure rise up, as if nourished into being by our desire.

She's wearing a beautiful red gown, with long curly hair like mine—and a vicious scar across her neck. Her dark brown eyes stare at me penetratingly, but then I see her lean her head back and laugh.

It's Martiya—

"Look at those red sheets," she smiles at me, pointing.

For some reason, I can see Creek and I in our act of lovemaking, as if I've become a part of her red vapor. We're beautiful together, our bodies entwined. But below us, the faded crazy quilt is stained with a spot of blood. My blood.

"Your lover has tasted you," Martiya says in triumph with folded arms. "Now you are a woman, a *Thagarni,* like me."

She holds up the ruby stone in her hand, where it glistens with an inflamed glow. The star-like cracks at the center pulse menacingly as if the heart is on fire.

And all at once, I feel my soul get swept into the cracks.

## ❧ 13 ❧

I'm a red column of pure energy now.

I want to scream for Creek, for Martiya—for anyone to rescue me—but no sound comes from my mouth. I feel like a lost little girl in this swirl of crimson smoke, disoriented, and I can't help wishing there was someone here to hold me, perhaps even my mother, to keep me from this bizarre weightlessness. With that thought, I see the smoke begin to clear out a little. Forms creep through the haze, and I spy a candle lighting up a small space. Hoping it's the candle in our wagon, I pull myself slowly toward it, like a gentle breeze, only to realize that there's another woman there. She looks a lot like Martiya and me—but she's wearing a black and white nun's habit. Her lips move slowly, steadily while she rocks back and forth, as though she's chanting Hail Marys.

"A-Alessia?" I burst, unable to deny the resemblance between us.

The woman doesn't appear to hear me. But her lips halt

for a moment as she takes her time to glance over her shoulder, as if she felt my presence with another sense altogether. When she doesn't apparently see anything, she stares at her candle again and rocks slightly, chanting more. The room is small and seems to be made of stone, with only a wood board and a pillow for a bed, and the moonlight from a small window caresses her nun's habit. In the distance, I can see beautiful mountains set into relief by the moon's glow. I recall the letter Creek stole from the de Bargona's that said *Istituto Mentale: Montagne.*

Mental Insitution: Mountains.

But this doesn't seem like a typical loony bin. More like a convent in the Alps, not far away from the vineyards that border our camp.

"Alessia!" I gasp again. "M-Mom, I think I can find you," I promise, looking again at the mountains and attempting to memorize their shape. "If I follow that landscape—"

Just then, a bird flutters to her windowsill. In the moonlight, I can tell it's a blueish falcon, perhaps the same one trained by Zuhna, and it lets out a cry. The woman turns from her chair to listen to it, her body language indicating its presence is not unusual. She picks up a hunk of bread from a plate near her candle and sets it on the windowsill for the falcon to eat. But when the falcon ignores her to look straight at me and utters a hoarse call, the woman swivels and stares in my direction. Her eyes squint, as if she might actually be perceiving my outline in the candlelight.

Then her eyes grow wide.

She drops her plate with a crash and screams.

"Robin—ROBIN!" Creek cries as if summoning me from the grave. "What's wrong, sweetheart—did I hurt you?"

He's gently shaking me to get a response. As my eyes focus on him, I blink several times, delirious.

When I gaze about the wagon, I realize I've returned to my body.

"She's not dead!" I burst, hugging Creek with all my might. His warm skin soothes my rattled nerves like a balm. He rocks me slowly in his arms until I stop trembling. We are skin on skin—it makes me feel as if we're soul to soul—and I allow myself to fully surrender to his tight embrace. When I manage to catch my breath, I let go and glance at the stone around his neck like it's an instrument of voodoo.

"This heart," I say, pointing at it, gasping, "it-it led me to my mother."

Creek braces my shoulders with his hands. "Robin," he says seriously, "what did you see?"

I can tell Creek's worried by the flinty look in his eyes. Staring again at the ruby heart, I flinch as if it holds a bizarre movie screen.

"I-I went *inside* it," I begin. "The minute I thought about my mother, it somehow grabbed me and took me in a cloud of red smoke to where she is—with Martiya's help, I think. If I can trust what I saw, Alessia's in the mountains north of us, maybe fifteen miles from the vineyards by our camp."

"The *Dolomiti*," Creek nods, wrapping his arms around me again. "Those are the mountains the gypsies mentioned."

He clutches me like I'm his everything—as if he feared

he'd lost me for a moment—and I have to admit that I relish melting in his arms. It feels so good to be naked and needing each other, in exactly the same way.

"But Creek," I whisper in his ear, "Alessia's not in an institution like the letter said. At least, not the way we think of one. It's more like a convent of some kind."

"The convent for crazy nuns?"

Creek pulls away from me and gets off the bed, walking to the front of the wagon and grabbing our clothes. He hands me mine and slips on his pants. "That's what I heard the gypsy men whispering about while I was shoeing horses," he says, putting on his shirt as well. "It's a place where the church sends nuns who have too many—well, let's just say—visions."

Reluctantly, I sigh and slip into my blouse and skirt, following his lead and realizing this might be the end of our honeymoon for the night.

Creeks walks over and cups my cheek, sensing my disappointment. "We have to be ready to move again by dawn, Robin, through the gypsy byway that no one can see. Do you know where to go? Did your, um, episode reveal that?"

I shudder.

*Episode*—

God help me, I'm a chick who actually has episodes. Weird visions like the crazy nun of Venice. And for whatever reason —probably because he comes from a spooky trailer park— Creek seems to be completely okay with that.

Nevertheless, he stands tall and gazes at me, and there's an odd look on his face that I don't recognize.

"You're a *Thagarni* now, aren't you?" he says with a resignation in his voice that's heartbreaking, as if he knows he has to share my fate with a destiny I don't completely understand.

"Yeah, I-I guess I am," I reply, recalling Martiya's words. I nod heistantly.

Without warning, Creek's large hands ball into fists. His face darkens and he glares into my eyes.

"But you know what?" he says. "You're also my *wife*. And to my mind, that pretty much trumps everything."

In that rubber band way he can snap from hard to soft, he gazes down at the stone upon his chest, brooding for a moment, before I see his fists relax a little.

"Now come on," he sighs, nodding at the bed. "We'll sleep in our clothes for a bit longer and head out at the first light of dawn."

## 14

I wake to the smell of smoke.

And I'm coughing uncontrollably.

For a second, I pat my hands down my body, wondering if I've accidentally entered Martiya's realm and the ruby heart again in my dreams. But when I look around, I see flames licking at the edges of our wagon.

"Robin!" Creek cries in a hoarse whisper, hacking. He grabs my hand so hard it hurts. "Follow me—we have to escape. Now!"

With lightning speed, he tears us from the bed and feels his way through the wagon to find a trap door beneath the table —I should've known the gypsies would have a quick getaway hatch like Granny Tinker! Creek lifts it up and we drop outside to the grass below in the darkness. It's only been a couple of hours since we fell asleep—not even dawn yet—but it's pretty clear to me that de Bargona's men have found us.

Search lights scan through the smoke over our heads, but

we slither like snakes along the grass until we reach the woods and bolt for a tree.

All of a sudden, I hear a huge crash followed by the sound of gunshots and running horses.

"Shh," Creek whispers, wrapping his palm around my mouth, knowing I'm scared and it's hard not to scream. "Climb the tree."

Luckily, I have some experience from living with Creek near Bender Lake. I hitch up my skirt and scale several limbs in a flash. Creek passes me swiftly and gives me a yank with arms so strong that my boots are dangling in air. With one big swoop, he nestles my body onto a thick limb beside him, steadying my waist for support.

"It's okay, we made it," he whispers, and it's then that I recall his words from dashing across rooftops in Venice: *Most thugs are stupid—they don't bother to look up.*

I'm praying that's true, because as two burly men go from wagon to wagon, tipping them over or setting them on fire, then shooting their guns in air as a fear tactic to make people come out, I'm petrified their search lights will spot the other gypsies as well as us, high in this tree.

But no dice.

Gypsies are hardly strangers to harassment, and the people from the camp spread as fast as ants, disappearing into the darkness of the woods like we did. Within seconds, all that's left in the center of the camp is Zuhna. She stands alone in their searing bright light, leaning on a gnarled walking stick.

*"Dove si trova la pietra!"* one of the men demands. All I can see of him is a dark suit—and a gun.

But Zuhna doesn't flinch.

*"Non qui,"* she replies coolly, shaking her head.

She boldly picks up her walking stick and waves it at the camp at no one there. Several wagons are on their sides and a couple are in flames that reach high in the night sky.

I'm in awe of her bravery.

But when one of the men jabbers at her insistently in Italian and then walks up to Zuhna and hits her with his pistol, I hear Creek spit through his teeth: "That's it—"

And before I can get a word in, Creek is gone.

Down the tree and back into the camp.

He slinks in the shadows cast by the men's search lights as if he were made of darkness itself.

And as the same man hauls off and hits Zuhna again so hard this time that she falls to ground like a ragdoll, in short order, that man's head is knocked against his partner, who falls with him as well.

Zuhna cries out.

Not in fear, more like a warning. But it's no use—

I hear a loud pop-pop.

And instantly, my stomach sickens.

I want to hurl.

Though my hands are covering my eyes, I feel frozen— unable to breathe or think. Cautiously, I peek through trembling fingers at the two large bodies that are lying in the camp, their backs glowing in the search lights. Creek has Zuhna engulfed in his arms, and he's rocking her and smoothing her hair, speaking quietly. In spite of the horror of his violence, my heart goes out to him.

Of course he'd grab the gun and shoot those men!

After years of watching his mother's boyfriend abuse her in

childhood without being able to do a thing about it, Creek wouldn't let anything stand in the way of protecting a woman now.

And there's no doubt in my mind those men would've killed Zuhna.

Nevertheless, tears stream down my cheeks.

Two bodies—two men dead—who were willing to do anything to get the ruby heart from around Creek's neck.

Zuhna was right. It's already proved to be one hell of a burden.

As the other gypsies slowly come out of the woods to approach the camp, timid as deer, I scramble down the tree and run to Zuhna's side.

"Come on," I say kindly to her, grasping her by the arm and picking up her stick. "Let me take you to one of the wagons or trailers that wasn't harmed. You can rest while the men dig graves. Creek and I will clear out right away. If anyone tries to bother you, say you never saw us—you have no idea what happened to those men—"

"No!" Zuhna hisses back at me.

She rips her arm from my grip and grabs the walking stick, pointing with it at the meadow beyond the woods. "I will burn them right there—where they killed Martiya and her lover. Where they transgressed against my people."

The venom in her voice sends chills through my body, and I know there's no arguing with her. She yells a command in her gypsy tongue at her men. Within seconds, they're towing a burning wagon toward the meadow, followed by others who've lit old branches like torches. They pick up the men's bodies and throw them inside the wagon. I watch in horror as the meadow becomes an inferno, in the very same place where Martiya met her end.

And I can't hold back anymore—I lean over and vomit what's left of my wedding feast to the ground as the smell of burning flesh rises in the air.

Creek stands beside me, stoic, as if he's seen worse. His hand gently massages my back, but he says no words to soften the harshness of this…of *our*…reality.

"Go," Zuhna says, turning to me as I wipe off my mouth. "Go now. We know what it's like to have our camps burned to the ground. It's part of gypsy life, of being travelers. And de Bargona will never admit that those were his men. We'll say they were gypsies who died in the attack. If you want to free your mother," she taps the stone at Creek's chest boldly with her stick, "then follow your star."

## 15

F ree my mother?

By following the star…

Zuhna's words tell me the de Bargona's letter was right. Alessia *is* locked up in an institution, unable to leave. It's just different than the white walls and padded cell I imagined. And those star-like cracks in the center of ruby heart are all I have to find her.

Creek is hiking beside me in the darkness along the secret gypsy path. And even though I know he's tough as nails and can handle anything that comes our way, I feel strangely naked without Zuhna's wisdom to guide us—and without the handgun Creek used to defend her. But the gypsies insisted on taking the men's guns to fence through the black market so none of us could get caught or be traced to the de Bargona's, and also to make a pretty penny. Creek says they'll need the cash for new wagons and repairs, which is the least we can do for hiding us. We let the guns go.

Nervously, I roll the ring Creek gave me around my finger as we hasten by moonlight down the gypsy trail, with only two old coats that the gypsies gave us plus the clothes on our backs.

And a scarf over my head that says in gypsy culture that I'm a "married" woman now.

To a thief—and a killer.

Shivering a little, I can't help wondering if this is the first time Creek has taken someone's life.

When he taps me on the shoulder, it makes me jump.

"Robin, we've reached the edge of the vineyards," he says, pointing at the rows of grapevines that extend beyond us in the moonlight. "Past here, we start climbing into the mountains. They're huge—we need to know where your mother's convent is."

He slips the stone from his neck and hands it to me, silver necklace shining in the moonlight.

"Here," Creek pauses, "hold this and concentrate."

The stone is cold in my hands, but not nearly as cold as the feeling that still riddles through my bones.

"Creek," I whisper, because it's way too hard for me to spit these words out any louder, "there's something…you've never told me—"

"You *know* I love you, baby," he cuts in with a sigh, as if all I need right now is reassurance. "And our last name's Flynn. I told you the truth—"

"No," I interrupt, swallowing back a stone in my throat. "Creek," the heat rises up my cheeks, and I pray to God I don't hurl again, "h-have you ever…killed…anybody before this?"

Creek is absent in the dark.

I don't know how he does it, but it's as if his soul retreats to a silent dimension in shadows, like he was a figment of my lonely imagination all along. I can't see him in the moonlight all of a sudden among the trees, and it makes me feel like I've fallen down a black hole. Like I don't know who he really is— who *we* are—

But then I sense a warm kiss on my forehead.

"Only those who deserved it, baby," Creek whispers, his voice shrouded in night. "I promise."

The ruby heart lies in the middle of my hands, cool as the night air around us.

I've got my eyes closed, trying to concentrate.

In my mind, I picture Alessia with long, curly hair and brown eyes like mine. I should be imagining her in a nun's outfit, repeating Hail Marys in that convent so I can figure out how to find her. But for some reason, I keep wondering what life was like for her at Turtle Shores. Did she and my dad kiss there in the moonlight under the stars, after he snuck her out from her boarding school? Did she let her hair fall loose, tumbling like dark lace around her shoulders? Did they run barefoot together in the soft sand by the shores of Bender Lake and skinny dip, the way Creek and I did?

All at once, I feel a warm breeze through my hair, odd for this time of night on the gypsy trail. And rather than my soul being sucked into the cracks of the ruby heart in a whoosh, I feel like I've become a part of that tender breeze. When my eyes flutter open, instead of darkness, I see Creek in broad daylight by the lakeshore.

Only it isn't Creek at all.

I realize it's my dad.

He's a young man, astonishingly handsome back then, with wide shoulders and a shock of blonde hair, bleached by the sun.

A young woman, a teenager really, who looks just like me in a winsome yellow dress walks up to him with hesitant strides.

Behind her is the Conté de Bargona, wearing one of his perfectly tailored suits. His eyes are stern—dark and bottomless in their disapproval—as if he has a gun in his pocket and is ordering the girl's moves. Alessia pauses to close her eyes for a moment, taking a deep breath as though facing a death march. Then she opens them, lifts her chin, and walks forward in the sand with a pained look on her face, like she's about to make a confession.

I watch her prim, white shoes get soiled by the sand at the lake's edge.

Her tummy is swelled beneath her dress.

When she reaches my dad, she stands with her feet perfectly together, then twists her heels a little, as if she's about to click them in the hope of escaping with him to Oz.

But there's no escape.

Instead, the Conté de Bargona orders something angrily in Italian to her from the shore. Shaking her head, Alessia says to Doyle, "*Non ti amo*. I never loved you."

And she firmly grips his hand.

"So this means goodbye."

Even so, the way she gazes into Doyle's eyes is the stuff love songs are made of. Her face is all heartbreak, all longing —and it's then that I see a peculiar mist leave her chest and surround my father's hand. It's as thin as cigarette smoke, but it clings to him like a ghost. Though her eyes are focused on Doyle, I watch them become dim—as flat as Zuhna's.

And I feel my breath hitch.

Even though my mind argues it's impossible, I can't deny what I see.

Alessia's soul has left her body to swirl around what my father holds in his hand. Taking refuge in the ruby heart she secretly slipped to him, the most precious treasure that the de Bargona family owned.

In giving him the stone, she gave him *herself*.

That's where Alessia really is—not within her body inside a nun's habit, or locked up in an old convent. *That's* why it was so important to my dad to steal back the box in our old home in Cincinnati that had been foreclosed. Because it held the ruby stone—and the love of his life.

My mind is reeling.

Doyle always said, even through his partially-paralyzed slur from his recent stroke, that Alessia was in the box. No wonder he kept talking to her in his dreams—she was really there!

But how is this possible? How does she breathe, eat, pray, keep functioning?

The same way I do, I guess—like I am now when I'm having an "episode," where my soul seems suspended from my body, but my body continues.

It's sort of like a seizure, I imagine. Only for her it lasts much longer. Perhaps even forever…

I turn my gaze once again to the lakeshore. The two lovers shake hands, nothing more, for the last time. Before I see Alessia let go of Doyle's grip, she drops her gaze and lightly touches her belly. Then she withdraws her hand without shedding a single tear, turns on her heels, and walks mechanically back to the Conté de Bargona, as if she were marching into the depths of the ocean to drown. He simply folds his arms and waits for her with an arrogant smile.

*Kill him!*

The ruby heart hisses to me.

*Make him pay for what he does.*

*He destroys everything.*

The stone has become hot in my hands and I drop it to the ground, my eyes blinking open in pain.

I'm waving my hands in the air, already feeling the blisters form on my palms.

"She's here!" I gasp, blowing on my skin.

I gaze at Creek in the darkness, my body trembling from what I've witnessed.

"Her soul—it's *in* this stone, Creek. Just like Martiya."

"But you said she isn't dead," Creek replies, uneasy. "How can she be inside—"

"I don't know," I shake my head. "I think it's because her heart was broken. Maybe beyond repair, after losing my dad and her baby."

"So Martiya protects her," Creek nods, studying the stone on the ground. "Protects what's left of her cracked spirit."

In the moonlight, we can see that the stone has become so hot in Martiya's rage that the leaves around it have begun to smoke.

"C-Creek," I stutter, deeply intimidated by what I've seen, "she wants me to…kill…him."

"Who?"

"Martiya," I confess. "She wants me to kill the Conté de Bargona."

## 16

"**N**o!" Creek cries out in the dim light, shocking me awake. "Don't hurt her! Don't you dare hit Caroline…"

We'd decided after miles of walking last night, and barely being able to see, to bed down along the gypsy trail till dawn. But in the hush of sunrise, Creek is standing over me in the woods, taking swings.

At no one I can see.

I bolt to my feet and swiftly back up, fearing the brutal force of his blows.

"Creek," I whisper in a hoarse voice, not wanting to give away our whereabouts, "it's okay, you're having a bad dream!"

He doesn't appear to hear me and throws a high kick, as though aiming at someone's head. When his boot lands hard against a tree, it jolts him awake. His eyes blink rapidly, confused and beginning to focus.

What I see next I've never witnessed before since meeting

him. Creek's typical wolf-like gaze is gone. And in his eyes is the horror of a child…

He's ten years old again, watching his mom's boyfriend beat her.

Welcome to Creek's childhood.

His mom's boyfriend was the guy who burned Creek and his brother Dooley with cigarettes and lighters, just for kicks. Carved designs into their skin with a knife to watch them scream. The same man who got Creek's mother so addicted that she didn't see the rope burns from when he tied the boys up so they'd be "good" while he got high. Granny Tinker filled me in on a few snippets of Creek's past, so I might understand why he acts the way he does sometimes.

Yet all I can do is stand here, horrified and allowing Creek the space to realize that his mom's boyfriend is no longer here.

But I know it's a lie—

Because ever since he killed Creek's mom, that man is *always* with Creek. Trailing him, haunting him, bearing weight on Creek's soul, like the ruby stone that hangs around his neck.

I thrust my head between my hands.

We certainly have a lot of baggage, don't we?

"I didn't hurt you, did I sweetheart?" Creek bursts, fully awake now and desperately peeling away my fingers from my face. He wraps me in his arms. "Oh God, tell me I didn't strike you—"

"I'm all right, I'm okay," I nod, but in the pale sunrise Creek spies the tears that have welled in my eyes.

"Creek, what's happening to us?" I blurt, hearing the traces of dread in my voice. "That stone—Martiya—wants de Bargona dead," I point at his chest. "And you want your mother's boyfriend dead. We've already killed two people, and we seem to be careening down this bloody trail of vengeance—when we barely got married! What are we becoming?"

"No!" Creek grabs my wrists with a power bordering on pain. I feel his fingernails dig into my skin. "That's not what this is about. Fuck what Martiya wants! We're here to free your mother—crazy or not, she doesn't deserve to live confined for the rest of her life because she went nuts after losing your dad and you."

He steals a quick glance at the wisp of light on the horizon barely peeking through the mountain spires. He lowers my wrists and places my fingers on the ruby heart around his neck, clutching my hands in his big palms. For the life of me, I thought I felt the heart pulse.

"We're here to free *you*, Robin," he says. "From all the pain that has influenced your life."

I stand taller, staring straight into his eyes.

I know Creek means well, and I know he's right. Only when I see my mother, and at least *try* to let her know I'm alive and still love her, can I let go of the past—even if it doesn't turn out the way I want.

But I also know Creek has a boatload of pain he's never been willing to talk about.

"What about you?" I demand. "And don't you for a second give me Mr. Stone-Cold-Tough-Guy here. Last time I checked, your pain outweighs mine by a few megatons."

Creek says nothing, and it makes me want to scream. I don't think I can handle his silence yet one more time, and if he keeps it up I'm about ready to slap him—his lethal right hook be damned. But to my surprise, he takes a deep breath and leans in closer, tipping his forehead against mine.

"In healing you Robin, I heal *me*," he breathes. "I don't know where that asshole is who killed my mom. And maybe I'll never know. But if I can make one woman's life better, prove to her that love can be okay, that it doesn't have to hurt and it can last forever—well, then maybe I can prove that to me, too."

The sun has begun to dance a little on the back of his cropped hair, making him look like a scruffy angel. A very sad angel, with the weight of over 500 years of tragedy linked around his neck.

"We owe this to ourselves, don't you see that, Robin?" Creek implores. "You have a mom. You have a chance to not go around haunted for the rest of your life. Like *me*."

I'm stunned at Creek's admission, that he actually formed words for his pain. And in spite of everything we've been through so far, I feel closer to him than ever before. Like maybe I finally broke through his ice a little. My hands cup his cheeks, knowing how hard it is for him to let that side of his heart be laid bare.

"Okay," I nod before giving him a kiss. "Then let's get to Alessia as fast as we can, before de Bargona has a chance to figure out what happened to his men. We'll try to find her as soon as the convent opens, and then I swear to God, we're getting the fuck out of Italy. We'll take her with us, if she'll come."

"That's my girl," Creek says, brushing his lips on my forehead.

And just when he smiles without a hint of his usual glacial reserve, I spy the blue falcon.

It must be only around six in the morning as I follow the path of the blue feathers that appear, one by one, to lead us up a majestic alpine pass in the *Dolomiti* mountains. I know it seems crazy to seek after them like bread crumbs in some weird fairy tale. But when I consider my heritage, it's hardly the wackiest thing the women of my family have done. With each step I take, my boots avoiding the last patches of snow on the ground, I keep peering at the rocky horizon, hoping to see some sign of a rustic convent.

"Stop," Creek says, grasping my shoulder. He lifts the ruby heart from the chain around his neck. "I think it's feeling warmer."

I sigh, relieved that Creek can sense the stone's guidance, too. The blue falcon returns with an insistent call, making a broad swath around us in flight. Then it soars away and cuts through a fog bank ahead on the right.

Creek follows the trail of the falcon with his gaze, before it seemed to disappear in the mist.

"It must be over there," he points toward the fog, thick as a curtain.

"But we can't see anything," I challenge. "It's so hazy we might not be able to find the path. We could walk over a cliff."

Creek settles his arm around my shoulder.

"That's the point," he assures me with a half smile. He glances at nearby ridges with his usual watchful eye. "They probably built a monastery hidden here centuries ago and defended it from these heights with soldiers when they needed to. Just watch your step."

I nod, imagining armed men protecting the church's interests. Drawing a deep breath, I press forward through the mist, my chest growing tighter by the minute. Not only from the altitude and nippy air, but also from the sick feeling that de Bargona's men might be upon us from one of those ridges if we allow the sun to get much higher. Surely he'll notice if his men haven't returned by noon, and then he'll send more looking for us. The way I figure it, once I see my mother, we only have a few hours to hitch a ride on a remote road to Switzerland, where hopefully I can tap into my Swiss bank account again and catch a flight back to the states. Whether I can convince Alessia to come with us to meet my father back at Bender Lake is another matter. But one thing I know for sure: at least my heart will have come full circle.

And then Creek and I can finally start the next chapter of our lives.

The *married* chapter.

That word still sounds so lovely—and foreign—to me. A little like this gypsy ring around my finger. I twirl it a couple of times for good luck, and forge on.

Creek and I march a few hundred more yards deep into the fog until it feels like it's swallowed us whole. Moist particles strike my cheeks and spread cold fingers across my face. When my foot slips, causing me to teeter on a steep slope, I let out a tight scream. Creek grabs my hand, righting me.

"Don't worry," he says, "I don't think it's much farther."

"Why?" I reply, puffing. The air is getting so thin my lungs are straining.

Creek turns my shoulders to face east where I should see the glow of sunrise, but all I can perceive is golden-hued fog.

"Listen…"

I assume he means I'll hear the falcon cry again. Yet through the mist, I detect the soft echo of singing. It's a gentle chorus of women's voices, chanting as if to greet dawn.

"*Cantate Domino*," I mutter—the song I always heard the nuns sing every morning at my old Catholic boarding school. In this fog, where I can't see a thing, the tune feels oddly familiar, and all at once it's like I'm a confused sophomore once again at Pinnacle. I shake my head to dispel the shivers that are working their way up my spine.

"She—she could be among them," I stutter, just now aware of how nervous I really am. "Out in the courtyard, singing along with the birds in the trees, like I used to hear at old my school if you got up early enough to listen."

This realization makes me want to run down the trail and scream "Mom! Mom, I'm here!" And even though I fantasize that she'd surely wrap her arms around me and cover me in kisses, I know my instincts might sabotage our plans.

"Okay," I nod to Creek, "I guess this is the part where we act like poor gypsies who need a handout, and hope that we can spot Alessia."

"Remember," Creek says, holding me for a moment in the comfort of his arms, rocking me a little. "Whatever happens is okay. It's still *closure*. Tell her what you have to say with no expectations. To clear your soul."

I nod, trembling again. Not from cold, but because other

than a gypsy wedding to Creek, this is by far the biggest moment of my life. I'm going to meet my mother! I take in a deep breath and head forward in the fog.

I know I'm walking way too fast, and I'll probably trip, but my heart is racing even faster. I can sense that the trail beneath my feet seems to rise and then crest. A gust of wind blows past us and for a moment, in a gap that begins to widen in the mist, I see it.

I see her!

A woman who's my mirror image, with an oval face and big brown eyes, just like mine. She's in a wheelchair being guided by another nun. They slowly settle into a clearing beside an old building with a rustic wooden cross at the top. The nun situates her in a patch of sunshine on a small patio before kneeling beside her chair. She points up at birds in the trees to get Alessia to notice them. But Alessia merely stares at her lap. Her arm is slightly askew with her wrist awkwardly bent, and she makes no motions whatsoever—doesn't even register that the other nun is there—as if she's...catatonic. The kindly nun smiles and jiggles her to no effect. All of a sudden, I feel the heat rise to my forehead.

The crazy nun of Venice.

So this is what they mean.

She's stiff as a board—unknowable, unreachable.

Swiftly, I turn to Creek and clutch the stone at his chest.

"Mom," I whisper way too earnestly. "It's me, your daughter. I'm here! Can't you hear me?"

Alessia's crooked arm flops off her wheelchair. It could be an accident, and I'm hesitant to read too much into her actions. Nevertheless, with my heart in my throat, I watch as she turns away from the nun assisting her.

For a second, it appears that she might be simply leaning her face to the sunshine. But then she slowly swivels her head. And looks straight at me—

Tears are trickling down my cheeks.

"She hears you, baby."

When I glance at Creek, his eyes are moist and shining, too.

I've never once seen him cry—not ever. And it leaves me all choked up.

We may both have had broken mothers, but mine's *here* now, and that means I still have a chance.

But a chance for what?

I'm not quite sure she actually sees me, or if she just somehow *feels* my presence in her heart. And when I meet her, it could end up being too much—and Alessia might retreat deep inside herself, or refuse to acknowledge who I am altogether.

Before I can mull over the possibilities, Creek hugs me and whispers into my hair.

"You followed your star, Robin," he says proudly, "and it brought us here. Now let's see if it can bring us all home."

He holds up the ruby heart for me, and the cracks at its center twinkle in a burst of sunlight that breaks through the mist. I watch as the sun spreads over the patio on the side of the church where Alessia sits, seemingly ignorant of the birds and trees and other nuns. Swallowing a deep breath, I glance at Creek.

"All right," I say, giving him a fist bump, "let's do this."

The sun is higher now, patiently burning away the edges of the mist, and it's easier for us to pick out the stony trail that winds down to the remote mountain convent. Honest to God, I don't see a single road out here, so I have no idea how they get food. When we draw closer to the main door of the ancient building, I turn to check Creek's eyes.

I should've known he'd be all focus again, scanning the rock outcroppings for de Bargona's men. The trail evens out, and soon enough we stand before the weathered door with a heavy knocker, which I lift and let fall. It echoes a hollow sound through the nearby hills.

And no one answers.

It strikes me that they don't get visitors here very often.

Just then, I spy a basket beside the door filled with loaves of bread and a sign in Italian that reads *Carità*.

I assume it means "free," and I break off a hunk of bread and stuff it into my mouth, marveling at the coarse grains and Old World flavor, before handing a hunk to Creek.

He chews slowly, his eyes never leaving our environment. I rap the door again—harder. Before long, it creaks open, but all I can see behind it is a wedge of darkness.

"*Silenzio!*" a stern voice warns before I can detect a face.

After an interminable wait, a hunched woman with grizzled cheeks dares to peek her long nose out the door, spying us with hostile eyes. She begins jabbering a stream of words in Italian like I've angered her angels.

"*Grazie!*" I spew out with a smile, holding up the bread—it's the only Italian I know. My desperation takes over in a blink. "Alessia?" I ask, sure my eager expression must look like a long-lost puppy.

The old nun lets out another river of Italian while Creek slides his boot into the door. I'm not quite sure, but I thought I heard her curse. With an aggression that startles me, she begins slamming the door on Creek's leg repeatedly with all her might.

"Ow—Christ!" Creek cries, glancing at me. "She's a mean one!"

He stops the door cold with his strong hand and glares at her.

That glare.

The one that can freeze any feisty nun—or member of the mob—into place.

"Now-now," he says, "you wouldn't want to hurt us poor gypsies, would you?"

The nun squints back at him with badger eyes. Though she probably doesn't understand his words, she appears to comprehend his intentions quite well. To my surprise, she throws up her hands.

"*Monaca pazzesca!*" she cries like a blasphemy, shaking her head.

Creek throws the door open wider, revealing a flock of other nuns shuffling to her aid. One of them carries an iron poker, and it's enough to startle me into taking a step back.

The older nun points at us with a long, gnarled finger and shouts "*Zingari—Ingles!*" like we must be witches.

Behind her, another nun—much taller and thinner but equally old—gives us a knowing sigh.

She holds out her hand.

"You are English?" she asks haltingly.

Despite the warmth of her smile, her fingers are ice cold as I eagerly give her a handshake to show we're friendly.

"Well, American," I nod. Then words bubble up inside me, and I can't hold them back a minute longer. "Alessia de Bargona is my mother—"

A collective gasp releases from the huddle of women, and I watch as they retreat a little as if I'd proclaimed I'm the spawn of Satan.

One nun holds up the cross of her rosary, seemingly to deflect evil. She points it at my face, then hesitantly leans forward to poke my cheek and jumps back, sputtering Italian.

From beside her, the old and thinner nun smiles softly.

"She thinks you are ghost," the woman says. "Like perhaps Alessia's spirit is haunting us."

"B-but she's not dead!" I gasp falteringly, as much to convince myself as them. For a second I'm scared. Maybe the woman I saw in the courtyard was the wrong person.

The old nun shakes her head.

"No, but she's not really alive, either."

Boldly, the old, thin nun removes the scarf from around my head and fluffs up my hair, judging the contours of my features before gazing into my eyes.

"*Sì*," she affirms. "You do look like your mother. But she was told *you* were the one who was dead. After birth. She kept having—what do you call them? *Visioni* of you growing up." The nun touches my cheek kindly, her fingers feeling warmer this time. "Perhaps she was not so crazy after all?"

Despite her gentle fingers, the coldest sensation ever winds its way along my skin.

"Th-they told her I was *dead?*" I stutter, shocked. I turn to

Creek to gaze at the stone around his neck. If Alessia somehow kept sensing I was alive, no wonder people thought she'd lost her mind.

But she was right.

"Here," the old nun takes me by the hand and waves at the others to make space for me to pass. "I lead you to her room. But I must warn you. We are people of God here. And our first concern is His mercy. If she does not want to see you, there's nothing more I can do."

"I-I understand," I reply, giving her hand a squeeze. My heart speeds out of control.

As I step through the door, Creek tries to follow after us, but her palm stops his chest cold.

"No!" she insists, shaking her head. "There are *no* men here. Not for *secoli*. Centuries. You must respect our ways."

Creeks eyes burn at her like blue flames.

"Fifteen minutes," he informs her—holy woman of the cloth be damned. His fists clench with a flash of knuckles that say he means it. "After that, if my *wife* does not return, there will be hell to pay. *Capisce?*"

## 17

The monastery is every bit as dark and damp as I expected, and there appears to be no electricity— just small torches that light the stone hallways with an amber glow, blackening the walls and ceilings with soot. I walk behind the nun who has my hand in her bony grip, my heart hammering fiercely in my chest.

This is it—

I try to heed Creek's warning not to expect too much.

Go with the flow.

But it's hard not to want to wrap my arms around Alessia the very second I see her.

She's a broken woman, I remind myself. She's been lied to and abandoned. She needs healing before she can ever acknowledge a daughter.

Measuring my breaths so I don't hyperventilate, I keep my steps in rhythm with the old nun's strides till we reach a dark wooden door.

The nun pulls out a large key ring from her pocket.

Seriously? They have to keep her locked in?

Catching the startled look in my eyes, the nun sighs.

"There are times when she used to run through the halls screaming." The woman lays her hand kindly on my shoulder, but I can feel her bones through my thin coat. "After she had *visioni* of you. She called out for her angel. We had to start locking her door to keep her safe from hurting herself."

"Hurting?" I ask timidly.

The nun nods. "She wanted to join you, Rubina. In death —and the after life."

I put on my bravest face.

But the truth is, this woman's words pierce me to the bone. Partly because it's obvious she knows my real name. And also because it's clear that my mother *did* tried to kill herself. To reunite with *me*—

Does that mean she wants me back, the same way I've ached for her all these years?

As the nun inserts the key and creaks the door open, I'm about to find out.

Yet what I see brings nothing but a clench to my throat.

Alessia sits, frozen, in a simple chair in her spare room, as though she hasn't moved in years.

Daylight from a small window casts upon her pale face. Her arms seem awkward and twisted slightly, atrophied and bird-like in their thinness. She looks like a woman whose soul left her body a long time ago.

"*Buongiorno, sorella!*" the old nun chirps lightly with the casualness of someone who's done this a thousand times before.

The fact that Alessia's gaze remains fixed on the floor doesn't disturb her in the slightest. She turns to me and squeezes my arm.

"You must have been adopted, no?" she says in a sensitive voice. "We have several *monascas* who once lost babies who were never the same. Be kind, *carissima*. Her heart may not be able to hold you right now. I leave you alone for a few minutes."

The old nun steps out and shuts the door—and to be honest, part of me wants to call her back. It's so strange to be isolated in this room with my...*mother*...who doesn't appear to recognize anyone, let alone me. What do I say to her now?

"I love you," I whisper, hating myself immediately for spilling words so fast. "I always did."

It's the first sentiment that came to my lips. I'm not in control anymore, and I know it, so I fold my arms to try to regain composure. I feel like I'm six years old again, alone in a huge mansion with nannies and maids who didn't give a rip about me, wishing I had a mommy who really cared. Tentatively, I step toward her.

"M-Mom—Alessia?" I stutter. Chewing on the inside of my cheek, I'm determined to tell her the truth, even if she never responds. "They lied to you, sweetie. I'm Rubina. And I didn't die after birth—I'm healthy as a horse. Your father ordered that I be given up for adoption."

My own words echo back to me from the stone of her room like I'm talking to a wall.

This is senseless, I know.

But God as my witness, I have to say it—even if it means

returning to Creek in ten more minutes with nothing gained. At least I'll know I tried.

Bravely, I step closer to Alessia and sit down at her feet, searching her dark eyes to make contact.

"Mother?" I say, hearing the heartbreak in my voice. I stroke her thin leg, feeling self-conscious and almost guilty, like I've dared to touch a rare and priceless statue. She doesn't flinch.

"Doyle—my daddy—he stole me back," I confess. "Don't you understand? He never stopped loving you, Mommy. Or me. He kept the ruby stone all these years. He kept *you*."

Impulsively, I grab her hands, but they're stiff in my palms.

Even so, I relish actually touching my mother. Her skin is smooth, despite the 18 years she has on me, and her hands feel warmer than I expected. I jiggle them a little to see if I can get a response. But her eyes seem flatter than Zuhna's—vacant, even.

This is totally hopeless.

I probably have only five more minutes, so I inhale a deep breath of defeat and let it go. I want to cherish looking at her. To simply linger and harvest this memory in my heart that's going to have to last me a lifetime.

Yet as I gaze at her, trying to memorize the curve of her cheeks and nose and distinctive arch of her brows, tears keep blurring my vision, in spite of my efforts to hold them back.

Dammit—

This is the *only* chance I have to be with my mom, and I can't even see well enough to store her image inside! She's become as hazy and gray as her cold, stone room that holds no personal possessions except for a bible, a comb and a ceramic wash basin. With a sigh, and painfully aware I'm torn and waffling, I decide to go for it and make every last second count.

Biting my lip, I stand up and give her fragile body a hug, squeezing her with everything I've got.

"Mom, I want you to know I love you," I say, certain of the clock ticking. "Even if you can't hear me, I hope you feel it—in your soul."

I rock her in my arms a little inside her wheelchair. It's like cradling a wooden board.

"And I know what love is now, because Creek loves me, too. Thanks to him, I repaired my relationship with Doyle. And he introduced me to all the folks at Turtle Shores who remember you. They miss you, Mommy. Creek brought me here to find you. He's my husband, now—we got married in a gypsy wedding, just like you did with Doyle at Bender Lake. Creek's my angel."

My breath halts.

I can't quite be sure, but I thought I felt her body tremble.

Just a slight tremor, almost like the wobble of a heartbeat.

"*Angelo?*"

She whispered the word, light as a breath, into my ear.

Yes, Creek's my angel! I want to scream. But I know I'd scare her witless. I have to take this delicately, with what little time I have left.

"Alessia," I say tenderly, taking her hands again in mine. "Creek's waiting for me outside. And so is Doyle, back at home at Bender Lake."

I swallow the sob that's trying to work its way up my throat, ready to stop any nun who attempts to interrupt me. I've probably gone over my time limit, but this must be said.

"I know this sounds crazy, Mommy. But if you agree to go with me, I can reunite you with Doyle. The love of your life. You can let your soul out of that ruby heart to really feel again—"

Are those tears I see moistening her eyes?

"*Mi Angelo?*" she whispers so softly I have to blink to be certain I heard it.

I'm trembling so hard now I can barely think.

"*Sì mama,*" I say carefully, oh-so carefully, daring to pull down the fabric nun's coif from over her head to reveal her wild, curly hair like mine. Hair that was meant to feel lake breezes, hair that was meant to feel a daughter's loving touch—

And just then, I hear a loud pop.

Shaken, I dash over to her window, where I see Creek in the small clearing beside the convent. He drops to the ground, blood blooming from his chest. In front of him are two large men who look like thugs.

The scream that erupts from my throat feels disembodied, as if it's come from the howl of a wild animal. Yet it fills the stone room with such blood-curdling echoes that it rattles my chest for what feels like eternity.

When I turn, breathless and frightened out of my mind, to face Alessia, the silence between us suddenly seems overwhelming—as large as any ocean.

Yet her vision has become flat as a piece of paper.

And that's when I hear the cold click of the lock at her door.

## 18

I am Alessia now.

And she is me.

We are as cold as stones.

Devastated, interchangeable. And unable to move, perhaps forever...

The Conté is very good at what he does.

All the de Bargonas have known how to keep their power —and destroy the *Thagarnis*—for centuries.

What made me think I would be any different?

Creek is gone.

The ruby heart is gone.

And so am I.

Whoever Robin or Rubina was—or could be—she's been erased, nowhere to be found.

In her place is a bruised and battered girl with zip ties around her body and a blindfold over her eyes who stands in the dark, tethered to a cold wall. She's lost the love of her life, and it's shattered her heart into a million pieces.

Beside her is her mother, whose own heart was crushed long ago.

Near as I can tell, we've been in this basement, cold and starving, for days. At first, I lingered in and out of consciousness, no doubt from the beatings we suffered when they took us hostage from the convent and loaded us, blindfolded and at gunpoint, into their vehicle. I have vague memories of hearing nuns screaming and then falling into total darkness, later being tied down here against a wall. Occasionally, I'd hear someone shuffle into the room to give us water or crackers, which I've barely touched. Yet time has stretched into something I don't recognize—hours of blackness and pain pass without rhyme or reason, with no way of telling one minute from the other, or day from night. But as the haziness from my head wounds slowly begins to subside, it dawns on me what de Bargona is really up to. This is his unique brand of psychological warfare. He wants to beat us into submission and make us believe we've been totally abandoned to his own custom-made version of hell.

And he's right.

I don't know if we'll make it out alive. Or even *why* we're alive—

Now that I'm becoming more alert, the same thought keeps circling around my foggy brain: Why does Vittorio de Bargona bother—why didn't he shoot us along with Creek?

We'd hardly be the first people he's buried. What's two more?

But then it hits me.

And I realize my precious, extraordinary and beyond beautiful Creek was a fucking genius. Like always.

Tears slip from my eyes and bleed through my blindfold in a stream, but I'm numb to their wetness against my cheeks. I'm so in shock that a nail could be hammered through my hand right now and I wouldn't wince. But I slowly piece together the truth.

Creek must have hidden the stone.

That's the only reason Vittorio would keep us alive.

Creek must have seen his men coming, and acted quickly.

I try to swallow back my tears, but my throat is too dry. I feel like I'm choking on gravel.

Even so, I realize the best way to keep from being murdered is to pretend I know where the stone is. For a girl who grew up acting her way through high society, this kind of charade used to be a walk in the park.

But do I have the strength to want to live that much? Without my Creek?

My body racks in sobs as I finally allow the tears to come full force, every part of me aching with loss. Until now, I stayed strong for my mother whenever I dimly rose to consciousness, stuffing back emotions to be brave for her sake. But what's the point anymore—no one's bothered to speak to us since we've been bound, and for all I know we might starve to death down here. Trembling, I reach out my hand to feel for from my mother, bruising my skin against the zip ties that fasten my wrists. Grabbing Alessia's fingers, I give them a squeeze to remind her that I'm here.

She doesn't return the gesture.

I know she's still alive because I can feel her pulse. Yet her fingers are as slack as a rag doll's.

"I love you, Mom," I say, squeezing her fingers again as I hear my words travel and grow thin in the darkness. "Don't ever forget that. No matter how many times they beat us."

And I smell him before I hear him.

A complex, leathery cologne that drifts into the damp room we're imprisoned in, about an hour's drive from the mountains. When de Bargona's burly men unloaded us from their vehicle, I could smell the sea air of Venice all around us, so I assume we're in the watery basement of de Bargona's *palazzo*, because they don't exactly build warehouses on pricey real estate near the Grand Canal. My feet have been wet ever since we arrived, and this place reeks of seaweed and algae and something else—like the odd scent of stale blood. As the precise footsteps of the intruder advances down the stairs, I'm reminded of the Conté de Bargona's stiff manner and tailored suits, and I'm almost certain it's him. His measured gait is followed by the lumbering echo of heavier men—no doubt his goons.

"*Ora!*" I hear him command sharply as they come closer.

The next thing I know, my face burns like I've been struck by a hot poker. One of his men has hit me—or perhaps it's Vittorio himself. But these aren't tears that seep through my blindfold anymore. It's blood.

My head is ringing, thoughts swirling and fuzzy again. I already hurt all over from the battering we received when they barged into Alessia's room after they were done with Creek.

*Done*—

Another sob crawls its way up my throat as I imagine what

they did with the love of my life. Could they have thrown him over a cliff, into the forest, or drug him back here and dumped him in the waters of Venice?

I'll probably never know. And that mystery will eat me alive until the day I die.

Why can't I just die?

Another strike batters my face, and I feel the blood pool beneath the skin on my cheekbone.

"Where IS IT?" the Conté de Bargona demands, but his words sound muffled in my brain, like they're far away.

We both know exactly what he's talking about.

I hang my head like I've blacked out to fool him, when I feel another strike.

It's in my gut this time, and all breath explodes from me like a pricked balloon. I grab my mother's fingers again to let her know it's okay—I'm so exhausted and in mourning that I don't feel much of anything anymore. But I do taste my own blood on my lips. It doesn't send me into the magic spirals the way Creek's blood did. But I savor it in my mouth, because this flavor is all I have left to remind me of Creek.

Please God, I beg, let these men kill me.

I want to join Creek in the afterlife. Maybe they'll shoot Alessia, too, and we can all be together again. We'll be whole, like Creek always wanted.

Cold fingers grasp my jaw, the way you see in movies when somebody's about to get their throat or have a bullet plugged in their forehead. But this is no movie. I should be scared out of my mind, but I feel as limp as a puppet on forgotten strings.

"Where is the ruby heart?" the Conté demands, shaking me until my head snaps back against the hard wall.

"C-Convent," I reply, a wild, reckless guess from a girl who's no stranger to lying. "Tucked behind a loose stone in the wall near the front door." Surely that's where Creek must have left it—or maybe in the courtyard, or beneath a bible someone left on a bench. It doesn't matter, because I'm certain de Bargona will kill us once he finds it, or even if he doesn't—and at this point that's all right with me. I think of my dad back at the trailer park at Bender Lake, how the loss of his daughter and the only woman he truly loved will probably destroy him. But that's okay, too. I struggle to take a breath, feeling the blood trickle from my mouth down my chin. Then we'll all be ghosts—and we'll haunt this asshole de Bargona until we drive him insane. With any luck, we'll have him begging for his own death in no time.

The Conté shakes my jaw again, then laughs.

It's a sick kind of laugh that bounces off the walls, changing its high tone to become low and hollow like the moans of a ghost.

"Rubina, Rubina," he says in an odd, rolling purr, "don't you know you should never have walked this earth? A poor bastard child with no one to love her."

A fire rises in my aching gut—

It starts in my heart and takes over my whole being, making every muscle spring tight. Roils of anger swirl in my stomach at the warped and stinging manipulation in his words.

He's a liar!

*He* may not have wanted me, but Creek did. And my daddy did. I may be beaten, and God only knows if my jaw is broken—because the pain that's pulsing in my face is excruciating. But I'm not going to let this demon from

Venetian hell twist what I know is the truth. He might've killed my mother's spirit, but no matter what he says, Creek's spirit lives on inside of *me*. I tasted his blood. I made love to him like a madwoman—we're one heart. And all I know is that Creek would never back down to this asshole, even if his whole body was racked in pain.

I shake my head, as much as it hurts under this man's grip, and picture Creek's eyes. The crystal blue way he loved me, without a hint of lies, as if giving of his very soul. The way he looked at me at dawn from that rooftop in Venice, like I was the most beautiful creature in the world and capable of just about anything—maybe even flying if I wanted to. It's tempting to let myself float away to that memory, lapse out of consciousness and allow this man to bring me to my eager, early death. But I know what Creek's defiant spirit would want me to do. Sucking up a deep breath, I bite down as hard as I can on the Conté's hand, letting out a rebel yell worthy of the red neck warriors at Turtle Shores.

"Ahhh!" he wails, waving his hand and cursing in a river of Italian.

The inevitable blow comes to my face again, but I don't care. This is what I'm made of, what the folks at Turtle Shores taught me. And I know Creek—wherever his spirit is—is immensely proud of me right now.

The Conté rips off my blindfold.

Blinking back blood, the room is as murky as I imagined. But through what's left of my blood and tears, I make out de Bargona and two of his big men in front of me. The dungeon-like walls are lined with old hatchets and scythes and other iron devices that appear to be ancient instruments of torture.

For someone as arrogant as de Bargona, they could easily be from some Medieval collection that he shows off to impress his friends. Except there's one more important detail: the edges of the walls are lined with fractured skulls and bones. And several of them still have remnants of skin and hair—

A disgusting hot stream of vomit explodes up my throat as I hurl onto the floor, my belly twisting from my wounds.

"You see?" the Conté laughs at me, pointing to the wall. "This is what waits for you if you lie to me."

I'm not able to wipe my mouth, so I swallow, feeling the stomach acid burn against my throat. I'm sure it's pointless, but in my last days of life, I have to know.

"H-How did you know I was here, in Italy?" I manage to form the words, despite my swollen tongue. "You attacked us the first night we got to Venice—"

"You're as stupid as your *madre*," he cuts me off, tearing the blindfold now from Alessia, too. Her eyes appear as dead as always. "Look at you two, just alike. She runs off with trash in America, and so did you. She thought I would never find out, but the *cagna* couldn't hide *la bambina*. And you—"

He grabs my face again so tightly that my skin burns.

"You have made me a *milionario*."

His smile is echoed with belly laughs by his thugs.

"Did you really think you could remove money from a secret account in the name of Rubina de Bargona, and I wouldn't hear about it? I have powerful friends, *mia ragazza*— and now all that money is *mine*."

I thrash fiercely against my zip ties, but I only manage to cut them further into my flesh.

"Th-that's my money! It came from my dad—"

Vittorio shakes his head. "You are dead, remember *stupida*? Right after birth."

The consequences of his words leave me gasping. I know my dad didn't want anyone to trace that money back to his own sketchy exploits. That's why he used my original name?

The Conté points at Alessia. "Isn't that a pity? And your *madre* is legally insane. I have the sole right to all of your money. Too bad your trash father didn't think of that. See? I have your death certificate right here."

He holds it up to my face where I can see the date: a day after my birth, 18 years ago.

"I don't care!" I hiss at him, casting a spray of spittle. "All money has ever done in this family is create monsters like you. Take it, you asshole—you can't have my soul."

"No?" The Conté lays my death certificate at my feet. In spite of my fury, it makes me shiver. "Take a good look at your *madre*," he says. "She didn't do as I said, and I destroyed her soul long ago. If we don't find the stone at the convent, I will kill her, too. Neither one of you is of any use to me, especially now that I have your *fortuna*."

He turns to his men.

"Would you like *per stupro*—how do you call it?—to rape these beautiful women before we go? They are all yours, *miei amici*."

The shock that bolts through my veins jolts my body like electricity. He would actually offer his men to rape his own daughter and granddaughter? His evil leaves me both frightened and reeling.

Vittorio de Bargona flashes his perfectly white, distinguished teeth, and I wish I could vomit on his tailored gray suit. But all I can do is kick and wail against my zip ties, feeling the blood trickle down my limbs.

Yet his two men trade glances and then stare at me without a speck of lasciviousness in their eyes. In fact, what I detect in the hardened faces isn't cruelty at all, but…fear. And that's when I get it.

It's one thing to kill me. But it's quite another to have sex —and possibly trade blood—with a known *Thagarni*. They're afraid of what might happen, that I might be able to control their souls.

"Ha-ha!" I cry, spitting at them. "Come touch me, you jerk! I'll bite you and swallow you whole you for eternity."

The Conté slaps me across the face so hard my cheek slams against the wall. The room teeters for a moment, and I'm actually grateful for the zip ties now that hold me in place.

"We'll see how much you laugh tomorrow if I don't find that stone." He gestures at the skulls that line the walls. "Don't worry, Rubina," he says as he turns to walk away. "You will be in fine company."

## 19

His breath warms my cheek, moist and soft.

Tickles my hair against my forehead.

God, how I want it to be Creek!

To be his soul come back to me for comfort. To remind me he loves me.

I know I'm probably dreaming, or hallucinating from exhaustion and my wounds. I closed my eyes for a moment, hoping to gather my wits and figure out some kind of desperate plan, even if it's totally futile. But whatever sleep I've fallen into now is disturbed by the sweet sensation of soft lips against my skin.

I'm afraid to glance up.

Because this man-smell I detect doesn't belong to Creek. His scent is wild—reminiscent of forests and campfires, pine sap and hardwood leaves and lake water, along with the natural, warm aroma of his skin.

But this scent is ethereal, laced with jasmine and patchouli, like Granny Tinker's wagon. It's a more exotic—gypsy—smell.

I know who this is, and he scares the shit out of me.

Bravely, I flutter open my eyes, heart racing.

Before me is a desperately handsome man with dark curls and bottomless brown eyes.

Bohemas.

I recognize him from my vision while holding the stone, and that reckless kiss in de Bargona's map room. He is Martiya's lover of old—that passionate heart that never ages.

And I hate myself for it, but I take a peculiar comfort in his presence, even though I know he's a ghost.

"Don't you bother telling me stupid, mysterious things," I hiss at him, in no mood for cryptic or puzzling messages from some lovelorn spirit. If he had any balls, he would've joined Martiya, the love of his life, in that ruby heart a long time ago. Or he'd cut these zip ties somehow and set us free right now.

He smiles at me, amused. Then he begins to gently wipe the blood off my face. I see it stain his ghostly hands— impossible as that may seem. And to my surprise, he takes a lick.

As his tongue relishes the flavor of my blood, I hear him sigh. Oddly, the color of his face and clothing looms brighter, and I swear I can feel the heat of his body near mine. He's so handsome beside me, it's enough to crush most girls' hearts, spirit or not.

He pauses to gaze at my mother and me, tilting his head to admire the beauty of what he sees. I know what he's thinking —that we could practically be sisters, and between my mother and I, we're flesh and blood echoes of his beloved Martiya.

How very, very tempting for him—but why should I give a fuck?

"Get us out of here!" I whisper loudly, rattling against our ties hooked to a chain against the wall.

But Bohemas only shakes his head.

"If your lover was really dead," he says in a low tone that makes me shiver, "don't you think he would be here right now instead of me?"

All breath siphons from body.

What the hell?

He can't be serious…

He's mindgaming me for attention. That's what all ghosts want, right? He's after another kiss, to give me a sweet bit of hope so I'll come alive for him in total gratitude—maybe even fuck him. I wrestle against my zip ties and wince, glaring at him.

"Th-that's impossible," I stutter, gathering breath. "I saw Creek get shot straight to the chest right outside of the convent."

This abrupt confession makes tears choke at my throat again. I shake my head to try and regain control.

Bohemas laughs. The sound fills the dark air around us and becomes deeper, as if falling through the wet stones.

"You think all gypsies look alike?" he presses.

I feel his ghostly fingers run along the embroidery of my peasant blouse, making goose bumps scatter across my skin. He traces the flowers near my cleavage where his fingers pause. "Some of them wear holy garments, you know."

My mind whips in confused circles, and I turn away. I have

no idea what he's trying to imply. He's just a goddamn ghost—crazy and fucked up as they come.

Persistent, his fingers work their way slowly beneath the delicate cotton of my blouse, lingering in the space between my breasts. I despise it that his strangely warm touch provides solace in the dark hopelessness of this basement. And the scent of him has changed, saturating the air with the man-smell of horses, blacksmithing, herbs and coal. He gently pats my breast. "They know how to heal a broken heart, Rubina."

"WHO?"

I turn to face him and demand he be clearer, but he's gone.

In his place lies a skull at my feet shrouded in black burn marks.

I let out a scream.

To think that Vittorio de Bargona's ancestor actually collected the skull of a man he'd incinerated out in a gypsy meadow sends vomit raging up my throat again. Dry heaves burn at my mouth, and I wonder if Martiya's skull is here somewhere, too. It's then that I realize all the bones down here are trophies to the de Bargona's of their power—and their brutal methods. I twist and turn against my zip ties and cry out my mother's name.

Like always, Alessia doesn't even blink.

All this time, she's simply stared at her feet. I try bumping against her to rattle her into some recognition, yet she remains stiff as the wall she's tethered to.

Doesn't she know we're going to die down here? Become more trophies for the de Bargona's sick collection? I wouldn't be surprised if the Conté keeps our clothes in his closet to sniff and remind him of his victories.

No! I wail inside, imagining our skulls lined up against a wall like all of his other targets.

It can't be like this.

This is *not* the way my life is supposed to end.

All this bullshit about being a *Thagarni*—some stupid Gypsy Queen! With no magic stone around, or Zuhna's herbs or Granny Tinker's crystal ball, what good is it? There's only one thing I know for certain—if we don't get out, we're gonna die here. And Creek would *never* forgive me, even in the afterlife, if I allowed myself to become another victim to an abusive man like his own mother Caroline. He loved me because I'm a fighter—that's the *real* magic I possess. He saw me knock myself out to provide for my dad and the people of Turtle Shores, and find my mom against all the odds in the hope of rescuing her. And when we were sleeping in that gondola in Venice, he promised he wanted me whole so our love could go on forever. As far as I'm concerned, that means kicking my way out to the very end, regardless of whether I succeed.

In a fury, I thrash again, feeling the ties slice into my skin, trickles of blood moistening my clothes. There has to be a way out. Has to!

My foot accidentally slips against the skull, totally creeping me out. It makes a hollow sound on the stones as it rolls over and cracks open a little, jagged as a knife.

That's it—

Bone.

Even after the inferno in the meadow where Bohemas died, his skull is *still* here. It's hardness has lasted for centuries.

Maybe that freaky ghost was trying to help me after all.

Carefully, I scoot the skull toward me with my boot. It rattles over the stones—a sick, hollow sound—and I turn it over. Lifting it up by the crack near the jaw with my toe, it's incredibly shaky. I take my blessed time, holding my breath. An inch higher, then another inch, until it's close—so close— to my fingers. Desperately, I push against the zip ties that bruise my wrist until my fingers…grab it!

I can't help trembling a little at the thought that this once belonged to a human being. Bohemas, someone capable of love.

Shaking my head, I force myself to focus on cracking open the skull farther, revealing a sharp-edged piece that already rips savagely into my skin. Wincing, I razor it across my zip ties anyway, harder and harder, until I'm bleeding like hell—and the tie pops free!

"Oh God, Bohemas!" I gasp into the darkness. "You did it! Thank you."

Instead of lingering in gratitude, I immediately start hacking at the other zip ties like a butcher. I'm a bloody mess from where the jagged skull piece has slashed my skin—but that's the price I'll gladly pay. As soon as I step my legs out of the cords, I turn to my mother.

I don't want to hurt her, but there's no other way, and we don't have much time.

"Mom!" I cry. "This is gonna hurt like a bitch, but we gotta get the hell out of here. I'm taking you home, Mama. Back to Doyle. Your angel."

I hack at her ties, too, but she doesn't wince.

"*Angelo?*" she whispers, hardly louder than a breath.

Goose bumps flare all over my body. I want to react, but I don't dare stop cutting.

"Yes, Mama," I reply, floored that she always seems to respond to that word, but unsure if it means anything, or if it's simply more of her textbook crazy. "We're going back to Doyle, your angel."

"*Angelo*," she says slowly, as if rolling the word over her tongue to see how it might taste. Her eyes appear to search the floor, but then she shakes her head. "*Angelo, dove si trova mia bambina?*" she calls out with a heartbreaking plead in her voice. Her words echo against the walls.

The only word I understand is *bambina*—baby. And the way she studies the floor is as though her baby is lost somewhere among the stones, among the skulls. Her body begins to tremble wildly, making it hard for me to keep from cutting her.

"Mother—*madre!*" I cry, stopping to shake her a little while my bloody piece of skull drips onto her shoulder. "I'm your baby, your *bambina!* Don't you see me? I'm here!"

Tears of frustration slip down my cheeks as I return to cutting her loose, my hands wavering in exhaustion. Even if I get her free, she's still as fragile as a bird! Where will we go from here, and how can I carry her? All of a sudden, an idea comes to me.

It's crazy. But sometimes that's how you have to handle crazy.

"Mama," I say sincerely, "we're going to go see your baby. Your daughter, *capisce?* But you have to walk out of here with me. To see your *bambina*."

Where, or how to get out of this horrendous basement, I

have no idea. But it's a start. As I finish freeing the cords from her arms and move down to her legs, I hear a gentle hum.

*Ninna nanna, ninna oh,*
*Questo bimba a chi lo do?*
*Se lo do a lupo bianco,*
*Se lo tiene tanto tanto,*
*Egli tornare anche lei?*

It's coming from Alessia. She's raised her bloody arms to cradle no one at her chest. And she's singing.

*Mi hai rubato il cuore, mia gioella.*

The shock of her voice—low and beautiful and piercing in its rich tenderness—knocks the breath out of me.

I've never heard my mother sing before.

Much less a lullaby, meant for me.

It's the same voice that wanted to comfort me, to guide me as a child and see me grow up. It's the voice I've wanted to hear all my life, to know she really *did* want me. I know I have to keep cutting, but in my heart, I can't bear to let this moment pass.

I stop for a second to lay a bloody, trembling hand upon her cheek.

"Mama—it's me, Rubina. I don't know what you're singing. I only speak English. But I *am* your daughter, and I think it's...beautiful."

"English?" She says puzzled. She tilts her head to the side as if listening to a far-off voice. "*Sì, mia bambina,*" she whispers with a slight nod, *"Americana."* Her head drops gently to her chest. She begins to sing again as though cooing to a child.

> Lullaby, lullaby, ooh-ooh,
> Who will I give my baby to?
> If I give him to the white wolf,
> For long time he'll keep her,
> Will he return her, too?
> You've stolen my heart, my jewel.

"No—no mama, I'm not stolen. I'm here." I pat her cheek again, but she doesn't appear to see me.

She's staring at a wall across the room to our left, almost hidden in the darkness. Her eyes are intent as if she spies someone there. For all I know, she could've spotted the skull of Martiya—or perhaps her own mother—and retreated deep into herself again. I shake my head at the grim thought and fall to my knees to finish cutting her legs free. Yet part of me wonders whether she ever came down here as a child. Surely she was curious about her family's weird treasures, the way most children are fascinated by morgues. To her, it might've seemed like a bizarre playground. Then the thought strikes me—if she ever did come down here, she might know where another door is besides the stairs leading back to the palazzo. As I manage to free her right leg and start hacking at the zip tie on the left, I hear an odd thudding sound.

It's Alessia. She's pounding on the stones with her fists.

Oh God, I'm hurting her so badly, she has to distract herself from the pain?

"Mama, I'm sorry. You're almost free! Just a few more seconds, okay?"

But even when I stopped cutting to talk, she keeps pounding harder with all her might. Her motion is senseless and repetitive, maybe what crazy people do to cope? I realize I'm cold, wounded, hungry, and scared out of my mind, all in one messed-up ball. But God as my witness, I could've have sworn I heard someone pounding in reply. It must be a ghastly echo.

Yet there it is again, from beyond the left wall.

I'm not at all sure that's a good thing.

"Mom, stop it!" I warn, as I manage to cut her last zip tie open. "We don't know who that is—"

"*Lupo bianco*," she whispers, cutting me off. Her fists keep pounding.

"White wolf," I nod, registering the words from her lullaby. Yep, crazy town.

"*Sì*, Mama," I nod to pacify her. "The white wolf has your baby. The song said so. Now let's go find her."

I grab her hand, my heart racing. These might be the first steps she's taken on her own in years. Slinging my arm around her for support, I guide her away from the stairs and from that creepy wall, praying that we might find some other door. I hear the pounding again like some wayward ghosts, and it scares the stuffing out of me.

"*Lupo bianco!*" Alessia cries adamantly.

She tears herself free from me with surprising force for a woman who can't weigh more than a hundred pounds. Her fists gather into tight balls again, and for a second I'm afraid she's about to take a swing.

"*Mio angelo!*"

Alessia points a shaking finger at the wall. The knocking has become so hard now its sound reverberates across the stones. With unsteady legs, she sets her feet carefully, one by one, forcing herself in shaky strides to reach the wall until she collapses against it. Then she starts wailing her arms on the stones with the fury of a caged animal, blood dripping from her wrists.

"*Lupo bianco,*" she insists, gasping for breath.

In an odd pause between the pounding noises, I hear a faint voice.

"Robin?"

## 20

"I-I can hear you!" I cry, barely able to stand from the shock. Leaning against the wall, I drum my fists madly against the stones.

I'm almost certain I heard Creek's voice, but could that be my panic talking? Like a wanderer in the desert hallucinating about water?

"Robin! Hold on!" he replies.

Trembling with my hands in pain, I hear a powerful thud, then another, as if he's throwing himself against the wall. All at once, it bursts open like a secret door—

And I'm flat on my ass, staring at…Creek!

For a moment, there are no words or thoughts. Just paralyzing astonishment.

He's a wreck!

Wrapped up tightly around his chest in bandages that look like they were made from torn sheets. On the upper left side is a blood stain rimmed in a strange green color that could rival the size of Bender Lake. When he realizes I'm fixated on his wound, he glances at Alessia and then at me, flashing his cocky, lop-sided grin.

"Jesus Christ, Robin, we look like a bunch of zombies."

"S-Stop right there!" I command, holding up a quivering hand and feeling like my heart is about to halt. "H-How do I know you're not a ghost? How can you possibly be alive?"

I'm hyperventilating and not making much sense right now, I know. But it seems to me to be a really important question.

"Oh baby," he says, his normally ice-blue eyes warming to an aqua liquid. "The bullet went straight through my chest, a hair's breadth above my heart. I faked falling down so they'd think I was dead." He runs his hand through his shaggy hair before his lip rises in a smirk. "It ain't the first time I been shot, sweetheart…or played possum."

I don't know what he said next, because I was up in an instant with my arms around his neck, kissing him to pieces. Ghost or no ghost, he's my Creek—and he's *here!*

"Ow-ow," he winces, recoiling from his wound. He takes a step back and licks my blood off his lips, then gazes into my eyes as if he were peering into a little piece of heaven. Carefully, he lifts his finger to trace what must be the massive bruises on my cheekbone and jaw. "Oh Robin," his hand lightly cups my cheek for a moment, but then tightens into a fist, "you have no idea how much I want to kill that asshole for what he's done." He leans forward to give me a tender kiss on the forehead, not wanting to hurt me. "But right now, we gotta go back to the gypsies. I gave the stone to Zuhna's falcon when I saw de Bargona's men coming, and I have a hunch she'll know where it is. They grabbed me and shot me before I could reach you." He brushes a lock of hair away from my eyes, his gaze full of apology. "And I passed out from the loss of blood."

Hesitantly, I lift my hand to touch his wound and snap it back, feeling like a doubting Thomas.

"B-But how did you survive?" I gasp, still marveling. "You could've bled to death."

Creek nods at me with soft eyes. "Those nuns—they weren't about to let me go. They came out in a line and stood up to de Bargona's men, waving crosses and saying they were going to give me a Christian burial or pray that his men and their families go to hell. You know those Catholic mob guys—deep down they believe what nuns say, and they figured I was dead anyway. After they left and the nuns realized I was alive, they lit candles and chanted over me and applied a cream on the wound that stunk like one of Granny Tinker's poultices." His eyes flash a bit of sparkle before he gives me a wink. "I think most of them used to be gypsies."

"But why didn't they call the police on de Bargona's men?" I blurt, half-grateful and half-angry at those nuns for letting them get away.

"They *did*, sweetheart." Creek sighs at my naivety. "But there ain't nobody in Italy who goes after de Bargona, if you get my drift. Now c'mon—we gotta bolt. I found this passageway from a small door by the street on the outside of the palazzo. The nuns loaned me their old truck to try and find you."

With that, Creek hoists Alessia into his arms and kicks the door open wider with his boot.

"*Angelo?*" She says softly, glancing up. "*Mio lobo bianco?*"

She appears frustrated, patting her nun's habit until she finds a pocket. Reaching inside, she pulls out a small blue feather and holds it up to Creek.

Tears well so quickly in my eyes I can hardly see.

The white wolf in her lullaby—

All those years, her song was her prayer for him to be her angel and come take care of her baby.

"*Sì*, Mama," I reassure her, my voice breaking. "He's Creek, our *angelo*."

Wasting no time, we dash through the doorway into a dark, secret passage, its damp ceiling oozing droplets of cold water upon our heads. As soon as Creek passes the threshold with Alessia in his arms, I grab the iron handle and pull the stone door with all my might to slam it behinds us.

And everything around us becomes black.

Sunlight stings my eyes as Creek kicks the secret door open to the street from the side of the *palazzo*, inviting the light of Venice to bathe us in warmth. Free at last from our prison! I swallow big gulps of clean air, blinking back glare, when I realize our feet are soaked in lukewarm water from a thin canal by the building that's overflowed its banks onto the sidewalk. But up ahead, on the street, I spy an old, dilapidated truck with a faint cross painted on the side. Creek nods at the vehicle.

"Run," he says, "the keys are in the ignition."

I dash to the truck and hop inside, turning over the engine

and backing it up in fits and starts. I'm a rotten driver, I know, but it's better than nothing.

In a flash, Creek has reached the passenger door and opened it to settle Alessia on the front couch seat that's so cracked and faded it looks like it hasn't seen use in fifty years. He slams the door and bolts around the hood to the driver's side, shoving me over to take the wheel.

"Hang on, baby," he says with gravel in his voice, "'cause I'm gonna drive like hell."

Fastening a seatbelt around me and Alessia, I nod my head. We both know this is no joyride—we could easily get shot.

He steps on the gas and the rosary that hangs from the rearview mirror swings wildly as he careens through tight alleys and side roads. Even though I know our fast getaway would scare the daylights out of most people, I feel a huge weight lift from my shoulders. At least we're not in de Bargona's dungeon anymore—and if I get killed out here, my spirit can rise free from my bones in the fresh air and sunshine! From the position of the sun over the Venetian buildings that are beginning to cast long shadows, I assume it's early evening, noticing the bustle on the streets as people head home for dinner. Signs blur past us as Creek steers a hard right and a left, and it's then that I spot a billboard advertising the airport. My mother jostles against my shoulder with another sharp turn, and I feel the blood still dribbling from her wrist that moistens my hand.

And an idea suddenly flashes through my mind.

"Creek," I urge, jiggling his leg, "what if we don't have to find the ruby heart to get my mother's soul back?" I realize the idea sounds preposterous. I push against his thigh harder. "Creek, do you hear me? What if all I have to do is taste my mother's blood to reach her. I was in her womb once, you know—we shared the same blood. That's got to be powerful." I hold up my mother's red-stained wrist to show him. "If you head to the airport, I can try it on the way."

Creek rounds another corner and slows down to head the truck into a dark alley before bringing it to a stop. He lets the engine idle.

"But we don't have any money, Robin," he points out.

My face flushes. I don't have my fortune anymore either, even if we did finally make it to Switzerland. I sigh and stare him straight in the eyes to tell him the truth. "D-De Bargona cleaned out my account," I confess. "He took everything, Creek."

Guess thieving comes pretty naturally on both sides of the family.

Creek's teeth clench, and I can see the muscles in his jaw begin to twist. The way his knuckles crease white on the steering wheel tell me exactly what he'd like to do to Vittorio de Bargona right now. Turning to me, he takes a deep breath and searches the cracks in the seat between us before he lifts his gaze. His eyes are so cold now in the center that they look like fractured ice.

And it's as if someone flipped a switch on his soul.

This is the Creek I don't know. That I'll never know.

Someone who grew up in the shadows of abuse and crime, who knows precisely how to do whatever it takes to survive. And who's ready to do just that at a moment's notice.

"I can *handle* the money part," he seethes, not needing to say another word.

We both know what he means.

Swallowing hard, I glance nervously around us. There are plenty of small shops and banks in this district that Creek could take in a heartbeat. And knowing Creek, he might grab de Bargona hostage and hold the asshole for ransom, if he doesn't kill him first.

Boldly, I swipe a lick of my mother's blood before I lose my nerve.

"Keep driving," I blurt, but I'm not actually sure those words left my mouth—

Because the moment I tasted Alessia's blood on my tongue, my soul escaped my body in a thin white cloud.

And all I can see around me now is a red, kaleidoscope of leaves, as if I'm high up on a tree limb somewhere, gazing through cracked, rose-colored glasses. Astonished, I reach out my hand, but it strikes what appears to be a wall. I touch another facet and then another, pounding on them in panic, but they're all as hard as diamonds, preventing me from going any farther. Frustrated, I turn around, only to see a scarlet flame erupt right in front of me that slowly settles into form.

It's Martiya—

She folds her arms and smiles, letting out a broad, deep-throated laugh.

## 21

"**Y**ou can't have her, *carissima*," Martiya glares, her voice a hiss of Italian that I somehow understand in English. "Until you *kill him*."

My mother is at her feet, curled into a fetal ball. Her eyes are open but glassy as obsidian, and she doesn't register I'm here.

Where *is* here?

A quick scan tells me we're in a bright red chamber. Above us, I can see a bleeding sky dotted with clouds washed in jewel-toned reds, as if I'm peering through crimson glass.

The ruby heart—

Can it be?

When I try to clasp my hands, my fingers pass right through each other.

I-I am spirit. A soul without a body, at least not the usual physical one. I'm vapor struggling for form. Yet the outline of my clothes clings to me like echoes.

"What have you done?" I demand.

Martiya throws her head back, scoffing at me. "*You* did it. You tasted another *Thagarni's* blood, trapping you here—where she is. After all, this is the Stone of Thieves, Rubina. Taking souls is what we do best."

"W-What are you talking about," I blurt, dumfounded. "Why?"

"Because he must die. It's our destiny to defeat them all and return the power to the gypsies."

Martiya points at her feet. She's wearing those odd Renaissance embroidered shoes with wooden platforms underneath them that make her loom tall above me, even though we're the same stature. Blinking, I realize it's not her shoes she wants me to notice, but a secluded, dark path on the ground beneath us, several feet down. It's then that I recognize why I've seen leaves everywhere. Zuhna's falcon has brought the stone to a tree branch near the gypsy trail.

Shaking my head, I try to sort out Martiya's skewed logic. "But your people travel in secret on this path all the time. One of them could easily spot the ruby heart and return it to their camp."

Martiya's lips slide into a smile. "Not if I don't reveal where we are. I can turn this crimson into our cloak, like the capes men used to cast over puddles for my delicate feet to cross. We are in no human being's hands anymore, Rubina. I will not let the falcon whisper our hiding place until de Bargona is dead—or I'll trap that bird's soul in my stone the minute it dies for a thousand years. You see, everything reveres our power. And no one's going to possess this ruby heart till we're free of the de Bargonas."

"Free? You want to be *free?*" I retort, flabbergasted. "Look at her! Look at yourself! You've been imprisoned here for over five hundred years, and you've kept her for eighteen. You don't want freedom—you're just like him! You only want power and revenge."

The scar on Martiya's neck from where her husband sliced her with a sword pulses as scarlet as her dress, seething in fury. Her eyes narrow at me. "Haven't you learned yet that love is for fools? Only power lasts, *carissima.* Ah yes, I forget you are young." Her ghostly finger lifts my chin, sizzling hot from the sheer force of her personality. "I have centuries of wisdom on you. Go ahead—choose love and try to walk free of this stone. But only *after* you make your lover kill him.

"My-my lover? What do you mean?" I reply, jerking my head away. I want to clench my fist and deliver a right hook to her chin, but I haven't figured out how to be as strong as she is in this form yet.

"You don't know? You can control him now—your pretty blonde lover." She brushes her fingers along my temple, where they burn so hot I have to turn my cheek. Then she sweeps her hand to Alessia at her feet. "Three *Thagarnis* in this stone have never occurred before in the history of the gypsies, and it brings a rare power. He has tasted your blood. Now you can make him do your bidding. It's our destiny, Rubina. Just think, he has no choice but to love you—and kill for you—whenever you like."

I recoil from her in horror. How could she dream such a thing, to treat Creek—or any other human being—like a puppet?

All at once, I realize what a fool I've been. Trembling, I

recall Granny's mysterious words written on the note inside the blue bird she'd whittled for me: *Beware of threes*.

I lean down to stroke Alessia's head, her hair still bound in the nun's coif, unlike the way she appears in the physical realm. But her form is as hazy as mist, her life force so weakened by Martiya's dominance that she's become little more than ether. "That's why you kept her all this time, in your ruby prison," I mutter, shuddering at Martiya's evil now. "Because you knew I'd come looking for her, and we'd make three *Thagarnis* for your plan."

I rise to face her, fists tight, in the same manner that I brazenly stood up to de Bargona. How ironic, the way they've become two sides of the same coin—both power hungry and wretched. But I'm not about to let this bitch rule my life the way he tried to. "What if I *refuse* to control Creek?"

"Then I suggest you get very comfortable with your new home," replies Martiya, folding her arms. "Believe me, Rubina —true hatred knows how to wait."

My cheeks flush hot, and I wonder if my soul has become as crimson as hers. No! I war inside myself. I recall Zuhna's warning in the meadow near the gypsy camp: *Will you lead the stone or will it lead you?* Now I know what she was talking about. But this is *my* life, my destiny, not Martiya's. And I can't let her destroy us all in her twisted bitterness.

"C'mon, Mama!" I cry. Impulsively, I bend down and try to scoop up Alessia in my arms, amazed that my spirit has formed enough strength in my desperation to cradle her against my chest, though she's thin as a wisp. "All you have to do is decide to go," I whisper into her ear. "Doyle's waiting for you. Everyone at Turtle Shores wants you *home*. This place is a lie! Martiya never protected you from your father; she imprisoned you for her own use! C'mon, Mama, we can be free—"

Jiggling her hysterically, I realize that the more emotion I muster, the stronger I get. Yet it's no use. Alessia lies motionless in my arms, her fragile limbs limp as a dead bird's. Undaunted, I set her down carefully and spin away from Martiya, determined to leave this stone and come back for my mother somehow if I have to. Drumming up all the life force I have in me, I feel my spirit swell into a ball of fury as I hurl myself like a comet against the stone's wall.

Sparks fly, and I'm knocked nearly senseless back down as the ruby heart flares crimson, as if its walls get stronger from my own rage. I swivel to Martiya, who's become all flame again, ablaze with power. She speaks to me through tongues of fire.

"Ah, *mia piccola*," she trills in an odd, musical tone, "who's the puppet now? You tasted your mother's blood, *principessa*. She became a *Thagarni* long before you. You can only do her bidding—and clearly, she does not want to leave."

Martiya's flame surrounds me in a sinister warmth that I fight against, even though my spirit is exhausted. She rocks me back and forth like I did with Alessia and purrs seductively in my ear. "Just one word from you to your lover," she whispers, "and I'm sure he will handle de Bargona quite effectively. I've been watching him for a long time, you know. Such a good little criminal. How hard is it, *ciliega*? Don't think of it as a violation. Think of it as a fulfillment of your purpose on this earth."

"No!" I shriek, I'll never turn Creek into one of her slaves, but she has me bound in her fiery grip as tight as a boa constrictor. "Mama, c'mon—you have free will!" I push at her wildly with my boot. "All you have to do is decide to go! We can leave!"

"*Ninna nanna, ninna oh, questo bimba a chi lo do,*" my mother begins to sing. In a strange, floating motion, she rises up and manages to sit, wrapping her ghostly arms around her knees. Slowly, she starts to rock. "*Se lo do a lupo bianco, se lo tiene tanto tanto, egli tornare anche lei. Mi hai rubato il cuore, mia gioella.*" As she sways back and forth, steady as a heartbeat, she hears nothing —sees no one—and remains absorbed in her own world.

But rather than sounding like a sweet lullaby, her song only sickens me to the core.

Because no matter how gentle Alessia's voice or lyrics might seem, it's now become the background music for our eternity in hell.

## ❧ 22 ❧

I sink to my knees and wrap my arms around my mother to sing along with her, copying her soft Italian syllables and letting them roll off my tongue.

I'm not sure, but I think tears are falling from my eyes, because I see a crimson puddle reflecting my own face back at me. A face of devastation.

Shaking my head, I swallow down a sob. I know fighting against Martiya does no good, as much as I hate her. Her rage has outlasted many weaker beings for centuries, and there's no one in spirit or on earth who can compare to her willpower. But I do have one hope left in my heart that Martiya can't sear with flames from my chest. If Alessia's prayers in the form of her lullaby all these years brought Creek to protect her baby— to protect *me*—then maybe her song can call him to me now.

*Lupo bianco,* the white wolf—

All at once, I remember the blue feather that was in Alessia's pocket. It's the same feather she used to pray with, and I snuggle my hand inside her habit to feel for its soft fronds, then hold it up.

"Creek," I whisper. "Where are you? We're *here*, in a tree along the gypsy trail."

The second those words leave my lips, I realize how foolish that sounds. There are probably thousands of trees on secret gypsy trails that weave throughout Italy. Yet I can't help singing with hope in my heart and drumming against the side of the stone, the same way Creek pounded the door to de Bargona's dungeon to find me.

"No!" Martiya rages. She ignites and surrounds us in a red storm of flames. Although I cry out in terror, as spirits we're not burned. It's like a bright red sun trying to overtake clouds —I merely see her glow all around us without consuming us.

And then an idea strikes. If we give her power as a threesome, then perhaps her energy gives *us* power, too.

In a crazy, reckless move—what've I got to lose?—I hold out my tongue to swipe a lick of her fuming spirit. Immediately, I see my skin grow rich with color, taking on three dimensionality, as if the force of her spirit makes my molecules combine into fleshier contours once again inside the stone. Quickly, I weigh the risks—by becoming skin and bone here, she might be able to burn me—but that's a chance I'm willing to take. I boldly swipe another lick and watch Martiya's image become hazier as her taste lingers in my mouth, scalding my lips and making my blood bubble up from a blister. The moment it does, rather than yelp, I sing louder, at the top of my lungs—and the sound reverberates through the ruby heart. All the while, I keep drumming on the sides of the stone for all I'm worth.

Furious, Martiya tears at me. Yet to my surprise, I'm as vibrant as she is now! Full flesh, and I refuse to let her life force bowl me over anymore. *It takes a woman to find a woman,* Zuhna once told me, and with that knowledge I stand up taller to Martiya, ignoring her scalds. She may have marked me for a scared little girl, but that was her mistake. I'm all woman now. And I've decided there's only one *Thagarni* who's going to rule inside this ruby heart—and that's *me.*

"Back off, bitch," I warn her, "unless you want to do *my* bidding! You thought I was too frightened to take you on? Watch me shove my own blood down your throat. Yeah, that's right, Martiya—because I'm still alive and you're *not.*" I glance down at my arm, which is growing fleshier in my rage by the second. "What happens if I knick my skin and make it bleed, Martiya? Huh? And force *you* to taste it? Real human blood?"

Martiya recedes to the opposite wall, her entire form ablaze. Yet in spite of her fierce front, I detect fear in her eyes.

That's when I know I've got her. While Alessia continues to rock and sing, I swipe my finger along the blood on my lip and stride right up to Martiya to grab her by the throat. "Eat it!" I cry, jamming my finger into her mouth. Her form burns so hot at my hands I have to let her go, waving the blisters from my fingers. I give her a shove with my boot and watch her topple from her high platform shoes to the floor. At that moment, I spy the cracks beneath her scarlet gown—the star-like fissures of the ruby heart.

*Follow your star,* Zuhna insisted, and that's exactly what I intend to do to escape. "Come, Martiya," I command. I may not be able to persuade my mother, but Martiya tasted my blood, and as far as I'm concerned, she's my servant now. "We're leaving this stone."

I grab her by the hair and dive for the cracks of the star, willing myself to become vapor again. In one loud whoosh, we're outside, hovering over the tree branch near the ruby heart like pockets of mist. But it's nearly dark all around us as the setting sun casts a striking swath of indigo and lavender hues across the sky.

To my astonishment, I see a silhouette.

It's a man perched in our tree, balancing precariously between two limbs and knocking in a fury on the trunk. In the dim light, I can tell his knuckles are all bloody. It's Creek! Below him, at the base of the tree is a small group of people, including my…my father? He stands next to Zuhna and holds Alessia in his arms, with my own body lying at his feet. Both Alessia and I appear unconscious, our limbs as limp as ribbons.

"Robin!" I hear Creek shout, pounding fiercely. "Robin, where are you?"

"I'm here! Creek! *Here!*" I cry. But though Creek searches the tree and appears confused, as if he'd heard a far-off radio signal in the air, he can't quite make out my form nearby in the twilight.

Letting go of Martiya, I swiftly race to inhabit my body again. The next thing I know, I smell the moist spring grass and earth beneath me, feel the throb of my heart and taste the blood that still dribbles from my lip. Trembling, I perch on my elbows and stare at my father, who holds the love of his life in his arms like a protective angel.

"Daddy!" I gasp, gazing at both him and Zuhna in wonder. "You're—you're here!"

Doyle is so stunned by my words that he nearly falls to his knees with my mother in his arms. Shaking, he sets her carefully on the grass beside Zuhna, where her cheek drops slack to the soft ground like a lifeless doll. Zuhna crouches to caress her hair, speaking softly to her in Italian, while Doyle kneels in front of me and cups my cheeks in his hands.

"My-My girl," he sighs with a heartbreaking tenderness, like I've come back from the dead. "You were almost comatose for two whole weeks. Creek had me fly here from Ohio to help find the stone and draw you out with your mother. Everyone at Turtle Shores pitched in for the fare."

When he kisses me on the forehead, his big hands holding my face like he'll never let go, I'm stunned that what felt like an hour in the stone was really a fortnight. And it begins to sink in how much my father has recovered from his stroke, both in speech and the use of his muscles. I stare straight into his eyes with apology.

"Oh Daddy, I tried! But Alessia's spirit is still in the stone," I confess breathlessly. "She was young when she was trapped. She hardly knows anything else."

I point at a red, misty patch floating near us in the air, the kind of weird phenomenon the folks at Bender Lake would call a "will-o-the-wisp," and return my gaze to Doyle.

"That's Martiya, Mom's ancestor who convinced her never to leave. Alessia's stuck inside the power of the stone."

"No," my father replies adamantly, shaking his head. He drops his hands from my cheeks and lifts my chin with his finger, gazing into my eyes. "The stone has no power."

At that moment, Creek spies me from his high perch on a tree limb and leaps down, dashing over to us with just a few strides. He scoops me up in his arms and hugs me so tight I nearly burst.

"Robin! Oh, Robin—it's you!" he cries. He squeezes me tighter and sways me in his arms before setting me to my feet. His blondee messy hair, tan skin, and almost golden aura envelop me, shimmering inside my every cell. And in that moment the world is mine—all *mine*, not Martiya's! The way he looks at me, as though I'm the very air he breathes, makes me wonder if Zuhna was right—by forcing us to go by *feel* to find each other, we became a part one another more than ever before.

"I-I heard you. Right here," Creek confesses, patting his broad chest that's still bound by bandages, "in my heart." His crystal blue eyes search mine for a moment before he continues. "We had to abandon our weapons in a river when the *polizia* spotted us, along with your dad's cell phone and GPS that betrayed our locations. We talked our way out of suspicion, and they moved on pretty fast. I can't quite explain it, but after that the way I found you was this strange echo of knocking, then the sound of singing, like…like a lullaby? It was this odd radar that led me to you." He sweeps my wayward hair from my eyes and steals a deep kiss, his tongue tasting the blood on my lip. "Blood on blood, sweetheart. I think that's why I could hear you. Because we're connected now."

"Yes, quite connected," a rich voice calls to us through the twilight, but it isn't my father's. "And I'll make certain your connection lasts forever—in death."

I hear the hollow scrape of metal as he cocks a shotgun,

but I don't need to whip around to know who's spoken these words.

It's Vittorio de Bargona. And he's found us.

Slowly, I turn to face my grandfather.

"You know how much I love beauty and symmetry," he says, staring at the dark stretch of trail that leads to God knows what gypsy camp. Behind him are four large men with guns as long as their legs, and in the distance I spy their van. The Conté holds up his weapon that glints in the last glow of the setting sun. "What a fitting end this will be," he continues, "for you two lovers to die in a gypsy hideout, just like your ancestor Martiya and her lover Bohemas."

Martiya's mist blazes redder, but she appears powerless outside the stone.

"No, let's make that all four lovers—two whole generations of reckless de Bargona women and their trash men. The stone must be around here somewhere, *si?*"

He walks up to Zuhna and points the shotgun at her chest while his men surround us in a circle.

"Zuhna, Zuhna," he purrs. "We go back so many years, don't-a we? To the days when you used to hide Alessia from me when she would run away as a girl, and claim you hadn't seen her. My men made sure you would never see again, didn't they, dear Zuhna?"

I shudder from the horror of his words, and the incredible loyalty of this gypsy woman, but Zuhna doesn't flinch. She stands erect, her dark eyes fixed on Vittorio's face as if she can see right through to his black soul.

"Yet though blind, you always seem to *feel* what many never see in broad daylight. Isn't that right, Zuhna?" The

Conté waves his gun at the nearby trail and trees. "I bet your falcon knows exactly where the stone is. Shall we find out? Either you call your bird to you with the ruby heart, or I shoot you here right now."

"No!" I protest, lunging for him, but Creek wraps his arms around me like a vise as de Bargona's men cock their weapons so fast, it renders me speechless.

To my surprise, my father squares his shoulders and stands taller, despite his weakened right side, to defy Vittorio—the very man who took so much from him.

"There's *no* power in that stone," he asserts in the deepest voice I've ever heard come from his chest. His words are slow and measured. "Only what *you* gave to it."

My mouth drops. Is he being brave, or is he bluffing again? Either one could get him killed—

"Then why has my daughter looked like *that* for eighteen years?" Vittorio points to Alessia on the ground, a shell of a human being with arms and legs splayed in awkward directions. "If the stone had not stolen her *spirito?*"

"*You* broke her," Doyle hisses. "But not anymore. Her heart —her soul—it's right here," he pats his chest. "And before you kill us all, I'm taking her back."

"Alessia," he leans down and caresses my mother's hair. "You're not gone, my love, you live inside *me*. I know you. Remember those moments that made our hearts come alive? The time I washed your silky hair with rainwater after our swim in Bender Lake? We snuck up and used Granny Tinker's rain barrel, and she got so mad she made us pluck chickens that night."

His smile stretches so wide it startles me, his whole face

warmed in light.

"Your favorite color's yellow. Remember how I bought you that pretty sundress? You said it reminded you of dandelions, only you called them *dan-dee-leoncinos*. And we danced in the moonlight as stars peered over the lake. They reminded you of the cracks in the ruby heart—flickering lights that you said were openings to your soul. How often we walked by starlight, hand in hand, or made love in the back of my old truck under a heap of quilts, counting the stars and listening to their whispers."

My father hoists her up in his arms again, his right arm trembling.

"There's never been a night I don't dream of you. Your face. Your smile. I know your favorite scent—lavender. Where you're ticklish, where your freckles are. Our daughter's alive, Alessia! She's right here. When your father sent her away, I broke the law to find her. I would've traveled to the ends of the earth to get our baby girl. I raised her, sweetheart."

He strokes her cheek gently.

"I didn't do a very good job, because I didn't think I could ever be worthy of her—or of *you*. My life's been a labyrinth of lies. But she has your heart, Alessia. She's brave and bold and beautiful, like you used to be. The you I knew—the *you* I know still! And she follows her heart no matter what. We don't need a ruby stone to prove our love. That *tresora* lives inside us. And every day I've breathed without you has only made those cracks in my heart bigger—bigger to accept more of you and your soul than ever before. The real magic we have is the love I have for you that will *never* die."

When my father leans in to kiss Alessia, his fatigued right

arm shaking to hold her close to his lips, something in me breaks.

Something I didn't really know was there, like a crust over my heart that falls away completely. Creek hugs me tighter, and I can feel his tears against my cheek, as if something in him cracked open, too.

This is it.

This is the end for us—

But at least we'll die whole, as a family, because we finally know what love is.

The night air is stilled by my father's confession. No one makes a sound. Not Vittorio or Martiya or even the birds, as though time itself has stretched to embrace this moment and hold it sacred in its powerful arms. My grandfather remains stiff, standing in front of Doyle and Alessia with his lips frozen tight, yet his gun upheld, as if stunned.

"Such foolish words!" he finally breaks, crushing the quiet. He steps up to my dad and swings the butt of his shotgun at his head, making him fall to the ground in a heap with my mother in his arms. "She doesn't hear you, you *idiota!*" He shouts at Doyle. Then he turns to glare at Zuhna. "Either give me the stone, or I shoot you all right now."

"Are you really so *stupido*, Vittorio?" Zuhna's lips curl into a half-smile. "I hope, for your sake, you are not afraid of ghosts." With that, she lifts a finger to the wind, as though she can feel something on the breeze. Then she nods and points at the tree on the gypsy trail that holds the ruby heart.

Strangely, a white mist hovers over the branches. As it begins to float toward my father, it takes on a luminescent, golden color. In the darkening sky, I can make out the form of a woman wearing a yellow sundress and simple, white shoes. Her dark, curly hair spills over her shoulders, appearing windblown, and her arms are outstretched. The nearer she advances to Doyle, the louder I can her words.

"*È davvero lei? Il mio amore?*"

De Bargona's men lift their gaze to the sky and instantly take several steps back, murmuring in Italian. One of them exclaims "*Madone di mia!*" and crosses himself before he points his shotgun at the apparition.

"*Non essere stupido!*" Vittorio cries at them, gesturing at the tree. "Go get the stone! *Ora!*"

Martiya's mist by the woods swirls to become a howling wind. "*Basta!*" she hisses, rushing toward the stone in a stream of sparks. Within seconds, pine needles on the tree erupt into flames. De Bargona's men begin cursing and crying out for God's mercy in sprays of Italian. But as Martiya's glowing presence become brighter, they wail at the top of their lungs. The men turn to dash away in fear.

"*Traditores!* I kill you—you traitors and your families!" Vittorio cries, uselessly shooting at them as they weave, zig-zag style, from his bullets and dive into the darkness of the woods. A couple of men dropped their weapons in the rush. In a flash, Creek grabs them and then runs toward my grandfather with his gun cocked, tossing one to Doyle. My father stands up and points it at Vittorio. Swiftly, Creek goes to the woods to fetch the ruby heart from its perch before it's engulfed in flames. As he returns, he holds the stone up by its necklace like a spoil of war.

"Kill him now!" Martiya demands, her rage casting sparks in the sky like fireworks. "It's our destiny!"

Despite her vehement red display, my father ignores her.

Instead, he leans down to kiss Alessia's limp body again on the ground. Her spirit hovers near him for a moment, floating like a golden angel, and then with a whooshing sound disappears into her physical chest. A warm glow settles upon her for a few seconds. She wraps her arms around Doyle, her skin fading back to a more human color in the twilight.

"Now's your chance! Destroy him!" Martiya fumes.

"She's been through enough—*we've* been through enough!" Doyle retorts, caressing Alessia's hair. "Don't you think this is the ultimate revenge? The fact that he could never kill our love—"

"Yes, but there's one thing I'm going to kill right now," Creek cuts in with his shotgun raised, staring at Vittorio. "You want this?" He dangles the ruby heart by the necklace, then throws it to the ground. "Let's see how well you do without it."

In a blaze of light and noise from his shot gun, Creek fires at the ruby heart, breaking it into pieces.

And all I can hear in that moment is Martiya's raw, otherworldly wail like a siren ringing across the sky.

"Drop your weapon," Creek orders Vittorio.

Reluctantly, my grandfather lets it fall to the ground.

"Now take off your clothes."

As soon as the Conté fumbles to remove his shirt and pants, Creek nods his shotgun at his feet to remove his shoes and socks as well.

Then Creek shoots him in the leg.

Vittorio lets out an agonized scream and curls into a fetal position, clutching his thigh with blood dripping down his fingers.

"This is what you are now," Creek says, stepping forward to grab his clothes. "A crippled old crazy man who has to walk naked to the nearest town without any I.D. Who runs around trying to explain to everyone about some ruby heart that he thought once gave him power through a bunch of gypsy ghosts. Who'll rescue you now, Conté de Bargona? Your men have abandoned you."

Creek glances at the empty space where their van used to be, then up at the red glow of Martiya. "And near as I can tell, you're gonna be haunted by that bitch for the rest of your days."

Creek shoves the shotgun in his face.

"And you know part what I find the most amusing? All that money you thought you took from Robin. Well, look for yourself." He points to Alessia. "Your daughter's alive! And now she can prove Robin's alive, too, and they can claim back that account. So go ahead and shove that information up your Swiss banker's ass. That is, if they ever let you out of the loony bin."

Zuhna taps Creek on the shoulder.

"There's only one more thing, *miri mora*," she says to him.

Above them, her falcon flies along the horizon past the red, setting sun and circles in the sky. She holds out her arm, and the bird descends to her hand and chortles softly. Zuhna nods, listening for a moment. "*Devel,*" she replies. The bird lifts its wings and flies past Vittorio to the darkness of the woods.

And that's when we see them—

At first they look like shadows, except they hover in a line near the woods, their feet not quite touching the ground, for as far as we can see.

Goose bumps spread down my neck, and I take a step back and grab Creek's hand.

"*Te' sorthene,*" Zuhna whispers.

Slowly, the phantoms grow larger and begin to take on more form. One of them I recognize as the portly gondolier who helped guide us on the trail from Venice.

Another one looks like an old nun, only with large eyes and dark, gypsy features—perhaps someone at the convent who'd once befriended Alessia.

Still another is a young and beautiful woman with caramel skin and black hair swept up in a bun. She's wearing a demure, old-fashioned gown with an apron, and I wonder if she was a loyal servant to Martiya. Alongside them gather a whole host of other spirits taking on definition in the murkiness of the woods, each one with swarthy features and black eyes like Zuhna's.

These are the gypsies who were the friends and protectors of the de Bargona women all along.

"No! It's not enough!" Martiya cries to the company of ghosts as she floats toward Creek. "You destroyed the stone— we'll never get justice now!"

But then Bohemas begins to appear among the spirits, wearing his gypsy trousers and peasant shirt and that black mask he once wore to a ball long ago. Rising up from behind the other ghosts, he moves toward us and removes his mask, staring at Doyle and Alessia with the longing of one who's known a broken heart for centuries.

"There is no curse," he calls out to Martiya, pointing at the writhing Vittorio. "It's your hate that kept you prisoner all this time. You were a Gypsy Queen—a *Thagarni*—you could have sent your soul anywhere. And grabbed me by the hand to roam with you, to wander for eternity and sing our songs. But you chose a stone instead of me?"

De Bargona watches in shock as Bohemas grabs Martiya and kisses her so passionately that her fiery haze begins to transform back into her crimson ball gown. Martiya's beautiful face and features become clear as well, and the scar that was once a gaping wound at her throat starts to disappear. To my surprise, she appears youthful, almost vulnerable, and she gazes at Bohemas with confused, questioning eyes like a lost little girl who wants to find her way back home.

"Martiya," I sigh, "There's no more stone, no more queens, no more *Thagarnis* left anymore. We're simply ordinary women who dared to fall in love. That's the only power we need. Go, Martiya," I encourage her, pointing at Bohemas. "This man has been waiting for you for centuries. And if that isn't true love, then I don't know what the hell is."

In spite of Creek's shotgun pointed at Vittorio's face, my grandfather dives for the pieces of the stone on the grass like a madman, clutching them to his chest until Creek sets his boot down on his neck and swipes the pieces from his grip. Creek walks up and hands the shards back to Alessia, who gazes at them like the lost pieces of her own heart.

"*Grazie*," she whispers, not as a ghost but as a real, flesh and blood woman, despite her stark, black and white nun's habit. She stares at the shards in her palm and turns to look at me with a wistful, yet puzzled glance. Does she recognize me? I wonder. Her fingers tremble, and she holds up what's left of the stone to gaze at me as if I might be one of the ghosts as well. "*Il mio cuore*," she nods.

Just as she does, Bohemas stretches his hand out to Martiya.

"Revenge, *il mia tesora*, or me," he declares. Hesitantly, as though he's a bit afraid of what she might choose, he dips his head for a moment and closes his eyes. But Martiya steps forward and grasps his fingers with both hands. Startled, Bohemas opens his eyes and nods, then wraps his arm around Martiya's shoulder to lead their souls back to the gypsy trail.

As they disappear into the elongated shadows of the woods, I hear an eerie wail, like the call of a wild animal that echoes through the forest, followed by the delicate melody of gypsy violins that rise and fill the air. The spirits are celebrating her home.

Home—

Creek gestures at the Conté de Bargona with his shotgun to start limping toward the woods for whatever the ghosts intend to do with him. It takes time, but after Vittorio vanishes into the shadows, with my heart in my throat, I walk over to Alessia—to my mother—and grasp her hands that holds the pieces of the ruby heart.

"We made it, Mama," I say, cupping her fingers in both hands and bringing them to my cheek. They feel soft and warm, except for the cool stone pieces. I have no idea how much English she remembers, or if she understands that I'm her daughter at all, so I glance over at Creek. He gives me a confident nod, pointing at the truck the nuns had loaned him from the convent that's nestled in a nearby meadow. Taking a deep breath, I grab Doyle's hand and press his palm against Alessia's, linking my mother and father together.

"Now it's time for us to go home."

## 23

Light glistens off the gentle, lapping waves as the sun dips slowly over the water, painting the horizon a soft gold. Pastel hues warm the nearby trees, and I hear a bird call, long and slow, its cry echoing over the shore. My mother and father sit at little table adorned with a white tablecloth, candles, and vintage china. They murmur softly as they clink wine glasses and give each other shy smiles.

They're getting to know each other again, the way all lovers should—by spending quiet moments together on "dates" such as this one.

But we aren't in Venice anymore.

We're back at Bender Lake, and the romantic dinner is Lorraine's infamous fried catfish and cornbread with a side of green beans, along with the Colonel's moonshine poured into Mason jars.

Something tells me Doyle and Alessia wouldn't have it any other way.

Creek has his arm wrapped around me. He snuggles against my neck and he gives me a squeeze. We're sitting several feet away from my parents on the sand, watching them giggle over old times and recall secrets that only they will share. I see the fading light of the sun warm my mother's face, and if I squint my eyes, I could swear she looks 16 again—like that teenage girl who thought Doyle McCracken had hung the moon.

My father's eyes appear equally fresh, but the gray hairs above his ears and wrinkles on his forehead betray another story. Even so, it's easy to tell that the woman across from him is his whole world. His eyes twinkle with every move Alessia makes—especially when she picks up a hunk of Lorraine's cornbread and takes a bite. Her face registers surprise, as if she'd hit a tooth on a hard kernel of corn. She pulls the bread away from her mouth, only to find a gold ring glinting in the sunlight.

"Doyle!" she gasps, tearing up.

As if on cue, several old men with fiddles—the ones who always play at Bender Lake hoedowns—step onto the shoreline from the woods and strike up a sweet melody. Alessia glances at them and gasps, before returning her gaze to my father.

"Will you be my wife—again?" Doyle asks with a world of hope in his eyes.

Alessia covers her mouth and dips her head, but it's only to hide her tears. When she's had a chance to gather her breath, she leans forward to give my dad a kiss.

And to her surprise, everyone we know from Turtle Shores steps forward out of the thick trees to give them applause. The

Colonel and Bixby, Brandi with Dooley at her hip, the TNT Twins, and a host of folks from the camouflaged trailers that surround Bender Lake. All but Granny Tinker, with her usual long velvet dress and flowing gray hair, and I shudder to wonder what she's up to now—no doubt gathering newts and lichen for more spells.

Creek grabs my chin and pulls me close, indulging in a long kiss, and I can feel the waning sun warm our cheeks. Afterwards, I lean my forehead against his, treasuring the way the soft light makes his blue eyes appear as clear as glass.

"Alessia seems happy here," I nod.

"I think this is all she ever wanted," Creek replies. "Along with you."

I feel a shiver work its way down my skin.

We don't' really know each other yet, my mother and I, but I've discovered she remembers English well enough, and we're working on it. It's strange for her to meet her *bambina* as a full-grown woman, just a little bit older than she was when she gave birth. And Alessia's spirit has been cooped up for so long that in some ways I feel like I'm teaching *her* about the ways of the world and what it means to feel again. When we take solitary walks together through the woods, I share the beauty of spring flowers and the murmurs of the lake with her the way Zuhna pointed out the magic of the natural realm to me, letting it cast its gentle spell as we talk about friends we both know from Turtle Shores. I'm confident our relationship will grow the way it's meant to, in due time. Maybe not so much as mother and daughter, but as survivor to survivor, and even more importantly, as friend to friend.

Yet she and Doyle seem every inch the husband and wife

now, though they were only married "gypsy" style, like me and
Creek. We watch them at their dinner table as Doyle leans
over to whisper a secret into Alessia's ear, and she laughs the
kind of easy laugh that makes you feel all warm inside.

"So," Creek turns to me, "what do you say we leave these
two lovebirds alone?"

He stands up and gives me a tug to my feet. As the men's
fiddles fill the air with another light tune, Creek nuzzles me for
a kiss, his lips soft and inviting. We watch our friends from
Turtle Shores begin to sway in a slow dance on the sand with
the warmth of the sunset rimming their shoulders. It's a
beautiful sight that makes me sigh as Creek and I dust
ourselves off and link our arms together to start walking
home.

"Home" for us is no longer a tree stand with two sleeping
bags. We've "graduated" now to our own gypsy wagon, a lot
like Granny Tinker's, that the TNT Twins traded a portion of
their ammo for as a belated "wedding" present.

Memories come flooding back as Creek and I stroll down
the honeysuckle-lined trail, full of the aroma of pine and new
blossoms and moist earth, the same place where we first fell in
love. When we reach the opening in a glen and see the small,
round-topped wagon with a red roof, Creek hoists me in his
arms so fast it makes me gasp, and then I giggle.

"All right, Mrs. Flynn," he smiles, his eyes twinkling, "it's
high time we started our honeymoon."

He reaches to turn the knob and cracks open the door,
holding it ajar with his boot. I'm laughing as he wriggles us
both inside without managing to whack my head on the heavy
wood door jam.

"My goodness—you're an expert, Creek," I grin before he swallows me in a kiss.

"I'll let you be the judge of that," he breathes, nimbly carrying me in his arms to the back of the wagon. He lays me down on our soft bed covered in old quilts. I hear a brief hiss as he steps aside to strike a match and light a candle in a Mason jar on a small table, casting an ethereal glow around us and making our skin look warm—ripe even, like Zuhna said. When Creek returns, after zipping open his jeans to put on a condom, his warm hands seek my waist and lift my t-shirt slowly over my head. He buries his face in my cleavage as he unclasps my bra, allowing my breasts to spill out to the warmth of his breath. Then he takes a step back from our bed without uttering a word.

His eyes appear melancholy and hopeful at the same time.

"What? What is it?" I ask, propping myself on my elbows.

Creek doesn't give me that sly grin that always puts me at ease and makes light of any situation. Instead, in the soft candlelight, the fractures in his eyes—those cracks in the center of blue ice—seem all too clear.

"You're so beautiful," whispers, "inside and out. I couldn't stand to ever lose you, Robin. And I almost did."

His eyes are glued to me as he slides off his shirt and joins me on the bed again. He wraps his arms around my body and hugs me close to his chest, kissing my hair. Gently, he runs his hands down to massage my breasts, his fingers working as delicately as if I were made of tender spring petals. Yet I'm already on fire as he leans in to swipe a kiss before steering his tongue gently down my throat and cleavage to my nipples. He circles one edge of my breast with his tongue, then the other and back again, until I'm building in ecstasy. Between my legs, I tingle and even ache for him, my breath short and halting at times, so I seek to slide his jeans and underwear down over his sinewy thighs. The feel of his smooth, hard skin beneath my palms sends me reeling. We both kick off our shoes and the rest of our clothes, then fall together, releasing long, drawn-out sighs, like spirits who've finally escaped to some pure realm where only skin-on-skin and heat-on-heat rule the candle-lit night. As Creek's lips descend to my breastbone and work their way over my stomach to my navel, I'm moaning in want—no, *need*—and I feel his tongue travel down between my thighs. Already I'm bursting with pleasure, white sparks flickering on the backs of my eyelids—I didn't even realize my eyes had fallen closed. Clutching at his cropped hair, I pull him down to me as the rhythm of his tongue begins to drive me insane. He's still so gentle, swirling and kneading, and I feel myself creeping over the edge. My entire body ripples and rises with pleasure until I hear some animal part of me cry out.

"Not yet, Creek. I want to you to come, too."

I edge myself beneath his body and take him, long and taut beneath my hands, and move his tip between my legs, thrusting him into me until we're one. My legs wrap around him and clench in total greed, but to my surprise, he smoothes his hand over my hair and rocks ever so slowly, gazing into my eyes.

"Mrs. Flynn," he whispers, rotating his hips in just the right way to make me crazy. When he sees my pleasure, that half-smile finally works its way across his lips, making that dagger scar over his cheek sharpen to a fine edge. "How do you like being my wife?"

"Pure heaven," I smile.

With that, he rolls and writhes, his muscles as tight and twisting as the snake tattoo on his arm, sending me soaring until I release a cascade of breathless gasps. All at once, his thrusts grow harder until I'm somewhere between panting and screaming and clawing for more. I'm almost afraid of myself, grabbing and demanding everything he's got, yet trying to avoid the raw wound on his chest that's still encased in bandages. I clutch his tight biceps instead, rocking him against me and feeling the slightly upraised scar where I carved the word *Partners* on his arm.

"Partners," he whispers with one final thrust, his back arched before he falls slack onto my chest, where I embrace him so tightly I can hardly breathe.

"Forever," I reply.

The hush that follows, that long and sacred gap of silence with only our ragged breaths between us, is what I treasure most. Our hearts beat on top of each other like one person, throbbing wildly at first but eventually slowing down to a more peaceful rhythm as my hand seeks the tufts of his hair to curl between my fingers. I stroke his moist temple for a second, then glide my fingers down his hard cheekbone and neck and along the curve of his smooth back, kneading his tight muscles as he begins to relax. But when my hand reaches the bed again, I feel something stiff with a firm edge beside us beneath the quilt.

"What is it?" Creek asks, as if sensing the subtle change in my mood.

"Uh, I'm not sure," I reply, slipping my hand beneath the

folds of our bed linen to check it out. "There's something here."

Sure enough, my fingers detect a box. I grasp it by the corner and pull it out. It's made of dark, distressed wood with a tarnished brass latch. It looks like the kind of small chest Granny Tinker keeps in her wagon to store rabbit's feet, incense, and herbs.

"C'mon," Creek urges, "I want to see what mischief Granny's been up to this time. It's probably her weird idea for a wedding gift. No wonder she wasn't around for your parents' candlelight dinner."

Hesitantly, I creak it open with the same trepidation as if it were Pandora's box, fearing what types of boondocks voodoo I might find.

Inside, I notice the chest is lined with a rich, red velvet, and I spy a large note in Granny's handwriting. Picking it up, it reads,

Happy honeymoon, y'all.
Watch out fer the shivaree.

"What's a shivaree?" I ask.

In my mind, I imagine some backwoods prank on honeymooners—one that probably involves banging on pots and pans, and maybe an explosion or two from the TNT Twins.

Creek laughs. "Don't worry, sweetheart—if they try to kidnap you, I can take 'em on." His mouth slips into a crooked grin. "Sounds like fun, actually. Just make sure you put your clothes back on before we go to sleep."

I give him an elbow in the ribs. "You're still healing from a gunshot wound, Mr. Flynn," I scold. "Take it easy, okay? I can fight for myself."

Creek nods and swipes a kiss, but then I turn over the note and watch his face turn to ash. On the back, it reads,

*And best beware of ghosts who never rest.*

"What does she mean by ghosts?" I add. "I thought we left them all a couple of thousand miles away, in Italy."

But that's when I realize Creek isn't looking at the note. He's staring inside the box, at a silver bracelet that was beneath Granny Tinker's strange message. Woven through the links of the bracelet are little dried blue flowers, with the letter C stamped on the clasp. Beside it is a lock of blondee hair tied with a blue ribbon and a small stack of letters bound with twine. When I turn to Creek, he's all of a sudden as far away from me as the stars.

Once again, he's that guy I don't know.

That I'm afraid I'll never know.

And his eyes are a wall of ice, even in the warmth of the candlelight.

Holding my breath, I jiggle his shoulder.

Creek," I say gently. "What's happened to you?"

He remains silent, every muscle in his body tightening, for what feels like minutes.

"Goddamn her," he finally whispers.

Swallowing hard, tears mist my eyes. I know what C stands for—it's for Caroline, his mother.

But why on earth would Granny Tinker want to spoil our honeymoon with a reminder of the loss of Creek's mom?

Fishing around the box with my fingers, I discover that beneath the lock of hair and a few lake shells and smooth stones lies the ruby heart.

The necklace has been attached to the top of the heart again, and it appears that Granny must have somehow glued it all back together. For the first time, I realize the pieces that had broken off from the shotgun blast had cracked along the fissure of the star.

"Look, Creek," I hold it up to him, hoping to change the subject—along with his abrupt shift in mood. "Shouldn't we give this back to the gypsies? After all, it's their heirloom, the Stone of Thieves."

Creek's eyes appear troubled, and so distant that I feel a chill travel through my whole being. I grab the quilt and wrap it tight around our shoulders in a huddle.

"Granny Tinker would've sent it back herself by now," Creek says. "Unless…"

"Unless what?"

He gazes into my eyes while his jaw muscles twist. For an interminable space of time, he's silent, until he releases a long sigh. "Unless she thought we needed it," he whispers.

Grasping the ruby heart from my hand, Creek holds it up by the necklace and studies its crimson reflections in the candlelight as though the stone were a witness to everything he never wanted to remember about his mother's murder.

"But I thought my dad said the stone has no power," I remind him.

I watch Creek's Adam's apple slide up and down his throat as he drops the stone into my hands.

"Your dad is a goddamn liar."

"So are you," I reply defiantly.

I'm on thin ice here, and I know it.

The way Creek looks at me, from somewhere dark and far away, makes me fear I'll never find him again. And it sends shivers straight through my soul. It's as though he's gone—long gone—down into a black abyss from his childhood that he's never completely revealed.

"You say we're married, Creek. But there's a whole world of hurt I don't know about you. That door is closed and sealed tight. And Granny knows it, and you know it."

I hold the ruby heart by the necklace up to the candlelight again to watch it shimmer as it spins in little circles, left and then right, before it finally becomes still.

"Until we find out who your mom really was, Creek—why she made the choices she did and what happened to her killer —I'm never really going to have your full heart, am I?" I say as bravely as I can muster. "Not completely, anyway."

Swallowing hard, I realize we're at a crossroads. And this night could be our last if Creek doesn't agree with me—right here, right now—because I can't take another minute of living on the wrong side of his wall, and not having access to his whole soul anymore.

The wagon falls silent as a tomb, and all I can hear is the sound of Creek's breathing. He doesn't look at me. He only stares at the ruby heart I now hold in my hand.

Finally, he strokes the back of my hair before leaning his head against mine.

"I hate that fucking stone," he whispers, staring into my palm.

I feel his breath warm my temple as his lips press for a kiss.

"But it's time."

"Time?" I reply, my heart in my throat, throbbing hard.

Creek nods.

"It's time to open that door."

His words barely leave his lips when the door to our wagon swings ajar with a warm gust of wind, scaring the daylights out of me.

The familiar orange glow of a thin cigar lights up the back of our wagon. "Got some news fer ya, Mister and Missus Flynn," Granny Tinker smiles, her gold tooth gleaming in the candlelight.

Her beauty still astounds me, with her silky gray hair and Greta Garbo-crossed-with-a-rock-star features. She strides right up to us in her long, black velvet dress and matching floppy hat with a feather in it, and hands me a crumpled copy of the *Cincinnati Enquirer*.

Apparently Granny Tinker's undaunted by the fact that Creek and I are nearly naked, covered only by the soft folds of one of her crazy quilts. As she crosses her arms and taps one of her lace-up boots, part of me wonders if she's been listening to us all along.

Seriously? A newspaper headline warrants busting in on us during our honeymoon? Why, oh why, didn't I think to turn the lock?

Glancing down, I realize the paper is curled open to the *Business* page. Circled in red ink is an article that says in bold letters *Pasta Sauce Dynasty Hits Hard Times*. Scanning the first few lines, I read aloud, "The de Bargona pasta sauce dynasty has taken another steep dive on Wall Street this week after their patriarch and CEO was found walking alone and almost naked in a remote forest of the Veneto, living off raisins and babbling about ghosts. Though he's since been taken to a psychiatric facility for evaluation, the international company is engaging in a massive PR campaign to reduce the damage. There's no word yet about his mental health, but analysts highly doubt that De Bargona International will ever climb out of bankruptcy."

I'm sucking air, but Granny Tinker merely takes back the paper from my hands and blows a stream of smoke from her cigar that rises and collects around her, making her appear as hazy as a phantom. She opens the paper to another section and shows me the *Lifestyle* page, where the headline reads,

*Enrollment Drops Off Sharply at Pinnacle Boarding School Due to Rumors of Ghosts.*

After our eyes trace the words, Granny Tinker folds the newspaper beneath her arm.

"Looks like y'all will be paying a visit to Robin's Alma Mater soon," she says mysteriously, releasing more puffs of smoke that make me cough. Her shadow leaps like a spirit against the side of the wagon with each flicker of the candle flame. Reaching into her pocket, she tosses a small bouquet of wildflowers into my lap.

"Them's forget-me-nots," she points out in a raspy tone. But her renowned timberwolf eyes, translucent gray with a fiery yellow in the middle, are trained on Creek, not me. "I gathered them tonight 'cause the moon's full, and that's when their power's the strongest. They always been known to help people find a lost love."

Creek is no stranger to Granny Tinker's spooky ways, and he's not exactly one to back down either, so he meets her gaze.

"My love is right here," he states with defiance in his voice, hugging me tight. "No need to be disturbing the dead."

Granny Tinker narrows her eyes, leaning in to Creek.

"You ain't the one who's lost, sweetheart."

She picks up the silver bracelet from the chest on the bed and holds it up to us. It glints in the candlelight, losing a couple of its dried, blue petals.

"And until your mama's found, she's a damn sight far from dead."

With that, Granny Tinker hands Creek the bracelet and turns away, just as we hear the hoots and hollers and pot banging of the folks at Turtle Shores preparing for not one, but two shivarees tonight. I pity my poor parents as Granny Tinker strides through our wagon to the door, when I see her pause for a moment to blow our candle out. Only the orange tip of her cigar and her slow cackle fill the darkness, making the hair on the back of my neck stand on end.

"Follow yer star, darlins," Granny Tinker's voice weaves through the wagon, though she's nowhere I can see. "An' bring everybody home."

In another gust of wind, the door slams shut, rattling our wagon a little. All at once, the ruby heart begins to pulse and feel warm in my hand. Then it flickers with a crimson glow.

ALSO BY DIANE J. REED

FOR MORE IN THE ROBBIN' HEARTS SERIES...

Sometimes a great love won't let go...until you believe.

Available at your favorite retailer and at dianejreed.com

**This isn't just any PTA. It's Gangsta PTA....**

**Available at your favorite retailer and at dianejreed.com**

# ABOUT THE AUTHOR

*USA TODAY* bestselling author Diane J. Reed writes happily ever afters with a touch of magic that make you believe in the power of love. Her stories feed the soul with outlaws, mavericks, and dreamers who have big hearts under big skies and dare to risk all for those they cherish. Because love is more than a feeling—it's the magic that changes everything.

To get the latest on new releases, sign up for Diane J. Reed's newsletter at dianejreed.com.